RIVER OF DREAMS
A PRIDE & PREJUDICE VARIATION

J. DAWN KING

Quiet Mountain Press

River of Dreams: A Pride & Prejudice Variation

Copyright © 2023 by Joy D. King

Cover design: JD Smith Design

Cover image: Paige Lampson Photography

Edited by: Christina Boyd, The Quill Ink

All rights reserved. No part of this book may be reproduced in any form or by any electronic or mechanical means, including information storage and retrieval systems—except in the case of brief quotations embodied in critical articles or reviews—without permission in writing from its publisher.

This is a work of fiction. The characters, locations, and events portrayed in this book are fictitious or are used fictitiously. Any similarity to real persons, living or dead, is purely coincidental and not intended by the author.

Published by Quiet Mountain Press LLC

Follow J Dawn King on Twitter: @jdawnking

Facebook: www.facebook.com/JDawnKing

Or connect by email: jdawnking@gmail.com

Please join my mailing list at http://jdawnking.com for news about latest releases.

❦ Created with Vellum

AUTHOR NOTE

I use American English in my writing. Some words such as bore, sibling, and target are too modern for Jane Austen, yet they fit my needs perfectly.

Christina Boyd, my editor, is AMAZING! Because of her notes and those of my daughter (author Jennifer Joy), drastic changes were made to my initial drafts. Did I play with the tale a bit after they were done? Of course! Therefore, all errors are my own.

Please enjoy!

PROLOGUE

Late November 1811

Fitzwilliam Darcy's mare surged down the hill toward the stone bridge crossing the overflowing river. With every pounding hoofbeat, voices from the past haunted him.

"Keep away from the water."

"Do not get close to the water!"

The river had been angry before the dam breach. Now, it was perilous.

Kicking his feet from the stirrups, Darcy landed on the bridge and slapped the mare on its flank. Fear seizing him, he peeled his great coat from his shoulders, tossing it in a pile with his beaver hat, gloves, and riding crop. He stepped on the heel of his left Hessian until his foot was free. Pulling at his cravat, he attempted to remove his other boot. However, he was out of time.

The terrifying vision he had spotted from the hillside approached: Elizabeth Bennet and two children were in the water, a capsized boat behind them. Tree branches and limbs battered them from all sides. The young ones clung to Miss

1

Bennet, threatening to pull her under. She grabbed a log in all the fast-moving detritus.

"No!" Darcy instinctively yelled.

"Help us!" Her screams increased as the water pushed and pulled. The log began to roll.

Leaping onto the rock wall, he peered into the swirling water. His heart hammered in every pore of his body. He swallowed hard, yet his mouth was dry.

He hated the water.

But he deeply admired her.

Closing his eyes, he only had time to whisper "Dear God" before plunging into the frigid water below.

CHAPTER 1

Fourteen years earlier - Summer
"Father, we are leaving the North Road."

"I am aware." Gerald Darcy's eyes never left the business section of the circulating newspaper. When they departed their home in Grosvenor Square that morning, twelve editions of the *Morning Post*, the *Morning Chronicle*, the *Morning Herald*, and *The Times* were stacked neatly on the seat. The man across from him studied each word so intently that only one issue was completed by the time the carriage made the turn. The others would take them almost to Pemberley.

His father was a man of routine. Thus, this could not be a spontaneous or leisure detour. For Darcy's lifetime, when they traveled from their estate in Derbyshire to their house in London, the Darcy carriages stopped at the same inns unless business was involved. Gerald Darcy lived to increase the family coffers.

At thirteen years of age, Darcy was grateful for his father's silence. Instead of, *"How are you faring, Fitzwilliam?"*

he would hear, *"Stop fidgeting," "Will you keep quiet,"* or most frequently, *"A Darcy never acts in that manner."*

Peering through the back window, the smaller carriage containing his young sister Georgiana and her nursemaid, his father's valet, along with the Darcy family's man of business humbly followed the grander conveyance. Were they as surprised as he by this unanticipated alteration? He hoped that wherever they stopped, there was shade. The heat, added to the dust from the road, was intolerable.

He examined his father from head to toe. Often it was commented upon how Darcy's looks mirrored his sire. Already he was almost as tall. Both had dark hair. Deep blue eyes. Erect posture and attitude. Even their traveling clothes were strikingly similar. The only distinction besides their ages was that his father wore a mustache and a closely trimmed beard. Darcy had barely begun to shave.

Since his father did not deem his comment worthy of an explanation, Darcy studied their surroundings. Hertfordshire. Stately oaks bordered lush green fields. Small farm cottages dotted the knolls. Healthy cattle grazed in one area while sheep were in another—a narrow river wound through the acreage. The sunlight glistening off the water beckoned him to shed his black traveling coat to find relief from the heat of the day. He would never give in to his inclination, never rumple his polished exterior, especially in front of the man sitting across from him.

Besides, Darcy no longer entered any pool of water larger than his bath. The very thought of it made him shrink back into the seat.

When they stopped before a tall building, a sign identifying it as the *White Stag* inn, Darcy followed his father from the carriage. Once the smaller vehicle behind them halted, his sister's nurse hurried Georgiana into the building, followed by the rest in their employ.

Gerald Darcy adjusted his beaver and gloves. "I have business that will keep me occupied for less than an hour. I trust that you will act the gentlemen while I am gone." Scanning the street again, he added, "Remember who you are and the name you bear."

The insult pierced Darcy's heart. When did he not act the gentleman? When had his actions brought reproach upon the Darcy name? Swallowing the hurt, he asked, without thinking, "Where are we?" Immediately, he cursed himself for his unbridled tongue. *A Darcy was supposed to know when to speak and when to keep quiet.*

His father's eyes shot up and down the street. "Nowhere." Settling his eyes upon his son, he commanded, "Stay away from the water."

"Yes, sir." The familiar warning barely registered. Without thought, he asked: "Do you know someone here?"

"There is no one here worth knowing, Fitzwilliam, nor will there ever be."

Gerald Darcy stepped back inside the carriage. Within seconds of its departure, Darcy surveyed the market town closely. *Meryton.* He had never heard of the place despite having acquaintances from Eton who were from the shire.

Being left alone, even if the only living being on the street was a donkey resting under the shade of a massive oak, felt satisfying—as if his father viewed him as closer to manhood than the nursery. He wondered if any eyes, probably peeking out their curtained windows, noticed his height or status. Why, he could barely pull the lapels of his coat together the way his chest puffed out.

Across the street from him was a haberdasher, a pastry shop, a blacksmith, a milliner, and a bookshop. At the west end of the street stood a church with a small garden on one side and a cemetery in the back. To the east, the road forked. His father's carriage turned right.

Once the coach was out of sight, he walked toward the small stone bridge in the direction his father traveled.

Despite his father's warning, Darcy was drawn to water since the day of his mother's death. For a certainty, he no longer swam. To blatantly disobey his father's command for the sake of pleasure would have led to dire consequences. Additionally, the idea of entering a body of water where he could not see the bottom was…he shuddered. No, he would never swim again.

However, since the accident, an inner force moved him to study any lake, pond, river, or brook he encountered, searching for obstacles that might snare a lady's gown, pulling her under to her death.

This day was no different. Instead of keeping away from the river, Darcy approached. He was surprised and horrified to hear a childish voice barking commands from somewhere below the bridge. He peeked over the edge. Gratefully, the clear water revealed the rocky bottom barely a few feet below the surface.

"Heave ho!" A sprite of a girl with dark braided hair and sparkling eyes stood at the bow of a dubious-looking raft. Two older boys manned the oars while another attempted to tie a cloth to a pole fastened to the middle of the deck. The girl peered into the distance, her hand shading her eyes from the sun before looking toward the riverbank. Darcy's eyes followed hers.

There stood a lovely girl a few years older than the sprite. Her wringing hands and pacing gave evidence of her anxiety. "Lizzy, Papa will not like you taking his octant or map. You should come away so we can return to Longbourn."

The younger girl replied, "No, Jane. I am afraid we cannot journey to the Amazon to find the lost Inca gold without it. Papa will not mind once we return with enough wealth, and

Mama will never need to worry about hedgerows ever again."

Even with a rising fear of the potential for harm, Darcy barely kept from grinning. The little captain, no more than six or seven, had a mighty lisp. When she smiled at the other girl, he could see the cause. Her two front teeth were missing.

One of the boys spoke up. "Besides, Jane, Lizzy said we'll see monkeys and black jaguars on our way. I've been wanting to see a monkey all my life."

Another boy agreed. "Yeah. We'll get to see an elephant and be rich at the same time." The third boy grunted his acquiescence.

"Well, I do not know," the eldest girl mused. "Will you be home in time for dinner?"

That seemed to catch the three boys' attention. "Dinner? Yeah, Lizzy, we can't be missin' dinner because Cook was makin' her apple tart this mornin'. She may get mad at me and Johnny for stealin' biscuits from the coolin' rack, but she never gets mad at Bertie, and he shares."

The little miss planted her fists at her waist. "Robert Lucas! You would encourage mutiny? You can't leave yet. How can I sail by myself all the way to Peru? How can I find Pizarro's buried treasure? You promised you would help."

How bold for a child.

Once the three boys abandoned the raft, they ran from the scene without looking back to wave. The rocking raft pulled away from its mooring, leaving the girl alone.

"Lizzy!" the one named Jane screamed, rushing along the shore as the raft floated to the center of the river. "Come away safely!"

Panic began to rise in Darcy's chest. The girl was alone on the water.

"No. To reach the River Thames and the North Sea by nightfall, I must continue my journey. Take care of Papa, Mama, and our sisters. They will need your help while I'm gone."

Darcy had to intervene, but the thought of nearing the water, possibly stepping close or even into its depths, made his heart pound, his palms sweat.

Likely, there was a deep pool where the water turned. Forcing back fears, Darcy ran to the end of the bridge and leapt down the embankment, his long legs racing until he reached the river's edge across from the girl named Jane. With another burst of speed and without a care for his father's orders, his pressed trousers, his polished boots, or his own dismay, Darcy pushed through the reeds until he reached a path.

The raft hit the bank, almost bouncing the girl off her feet. The port side gave a violent shudder before succumbing to the mud. One by one, the crudely assembled timbers broke away to float down the river. Without a miracle, the girl and her vessel were going nowhere.

When the pole with the improvised sail splashed into the water, the young girl grabbed a wooden container before jumping to the muddy bank, where Darcy slid to a stop. She ignored his outstretched hand. Shaking water droplets from her skirt, she splattered some on his Hessians.

Regardless of his youth, he could see many reasons her journey, even as far as around the bend, would not have succeeded. Gratefully, she stood on solid ground as the last of the raft broke into pieces.

"*Drat!*" Looking up at him, she asked, "Don't you dream of adventure, being as rich as Croesus, and discovering what is on the other side of the ocean?"

Stepping from the river's edge, he took a moment before he spoke. "I...well, I must admit that I have never given the matter much thought." Darcy was surprised at the question coming from a girl so young. "It is apparent from your attempt today that you have seriously considered the prospect."

She huffed. "Aye! I have. I have been planning this trip for a full five days. Robby, Johnny, and Bertie Lucas agreed to join me for an equal share of the treasure. Silly boys, each of them. They sold seven hundred fifty tons of gold for an apple tart."

His inclination was to scoff at the ridiculousness of her plans. Yet, he admired her spirit. "Is your life so mundane that you sought escape?"

Eyeing him carefully, she said, "I know that mundane means dull. And, yes, my life is certainly very dull. Our father refers to our family as 'proud Boeotians.' Do you know what that is? It is a person who is dull, obtuse, and unrefined. My sisters and I are still under the thumb of a nurse who thinks she knows everything. Well, Papa taught me to read when I was quite small. He has many map books. I love to look at the pictures and dream of who lives there and what they are like. I know there is much more out there." Her arm swept into an arc away from her.

"You do not think you are full young for this adventure? The Amazon is thousands of miles away. The river itself is thousands of miles long. The journey is perilous. For the past two hundred years, many explorers have sought the gold with no success. What makes you think you would ever reach the shores of the Amazon or find the treasure?"

The girl glanced at him like he was a simpleton. "I have a map."

"I see." He wanted to smile but inherently knew she would not be pleased. "Might I take a look at this map?"

"Certainly." Opening the wooden box, she unfolded a scrap piece of parchment with a rudimentary drawing of

England in the top right corner with a somewhat hazy sketch of what must have been South America on the lower left. In the middle of the continent, *Amazon was* scribbled in capital letters.

"My father would be displeased if I took the original map. I made my own copy. However, even if I lost it or some thieving highwayman stole it, I have memorized all the important points to make the trip safely."

"What would you do if your vessel was damaged?" He gestured toward the wreckage.

She shrugged. "Papa says I swim like a shark."

His mother could also swim, yet that skill had not kept her alive.

"That ability cannot always save you. What about pirates? Are you prepared to defend yourself, your crew…well, your former crew, and your ship if you are attacked?"

Slapping her forehead, she again looked at Darcy. "I knew I forgot something. Do you have a pistol?"

This time he could not keep the grin from his face. "I do."

Nodding once, she stuck out her hand. "Very well, then. I am Captain Lizzy of the recently sunk *HMS Voyager*. I am recruiting crew members skilled in sailing, carpentry, and shooting. You will need to bring your own weapon. Mightn't you be interested?"

With little hesitation, he wiped his palms on the side of his trousers and took her hand, bowing over slim fingers. "I thank you for the excellent invitation. However, my path in life was set at birth. As you sail the world searching for treasure, I will learn to manage our family estate in Derbyshire as the firstborn son."

Her head tilted to the side, her eyes squinting in the sunlight. "Jane is the firstborn too. Mama expects her to marry a rich man so we will not be thrown from our house when Papa dies. Longbourn has an entail. Do you know what that is? I do."

"Yes, I know about entails."

"Well, I have no intention of living in the hedgerows if I can help it, and my favorite sister should not need to marry if she does not want to. Besides, I want to see monkeys and jaguars and sloths." She looked back to where the lone piece of raft bobbed in the water. "If you cannot come with me, then I will find someone else. According to my mother, I am persistent, which means that I do not give up easily. I will not quit until my dreams come true. This river is the key."

Rivers are dangerous! He feared the boldness of this child.

"You sound very grown up for a lady so young," Darcy admitted. "My father will be waiting for me. Now that you are safely on shore, I shall return to the inn." He bowed and then waved at the fair-haired girl across the river. "I wish the best for you both."

The captain gathered a fistful of fabric in each hand and curtsied. Her skirt was coarse cotton, like what Pemberley's kitchen servants wore. "Thank you for your efforts to rescue me, kind sir."

Walking toward the bridge, he turned to see if the little girl had followed. She sat on the embankment, her elbows on her knees with her chin in the palms of her hands. Without a doubt, she was plotting her course. He could not keep himself from saying, "By the way, elephants are in Africa and Asia, not South America."

"I know," she grumbled. "I had to promise them elephants, or they wouldn't come. Stupid boys!"

He chuckled. Had he ever been that motivated to set out on his own? Whether he had or not, he was a Darcy. Darcys were responsible, tied to the land of their inheritance. Darcys were as reliable as the sunrise and sunset each day. Darcys no longer neared the water.

He exhaled heavily. Unlike the little girl, the Darcys were dull.

* * *

Fortunately, he gained the attention of Parker, his father's valet, before Gerald Darcy saw the condition of Darcy's clothing. By the time the two generations were back inside the carriage, the valet had pressed Darcy's trousers to a sharp edge, and his boots were polished, removing all evidence of the water, the captain, and her aborted journey down her river of dreams.

"Did you find something suitable to occupy your time?" Gerald Darcy inquired.

The impatient glint in his father's eye and the heightened color of his face convinced Darcy to be cautious with his words. Gerald Darcy's anger simmered below the surface. A slight irritation would light the fuse leading to an explosion that would unbalance Darcy's world for the rest of the trip. "There were some children…."

"Ill-bred misfits, I imagine." His father jeered. "Darcys do not fraternize with the riffraff in these villages, Fitzwilliam. The less we have to do with them, the better our lives shall be. You did not get close to the river, did you?"

Darcy was even more careful with his reply. "I always listen to you, Father."

He hated being deceitful, but admitting his actions would have been more than he could bear. If only he had the freedom as Captain Lizzy to seek his own dreams. But he was not allowed, nor would he ever be.

Tapping the roof with his walking stick, his father commanded, "Walk on."

Darcy forced himself not to look back to see the voyager. Unless he did as his father demanded, there would be no peace on their journey to Pemberley and possibly beyond. The few times his father had given him the silent treatment, he not only refrained from addressing his son but the servants and Darcy's cousins were not allowed to speak to him either.

Darcy knew that obeying his father was the course of wisdom. The alternative simply could not be borne.

CHAPTER 2

End of October 1811 - London

Colonel Richard Fitzwilliam paced from one end of Darcy's study to the other. Finally, he stopped. "I have my orders. I have two months to train a regiment of green recruits, and then we are for Spain."

What a blow! Darcy's cousin, his closest and most trusted friend, served in His Majesty's army. Additionally, at the death of Darcy's father five years prior, Richard was appointed as co-guardian to Georgiana Darcy, a task made difficult by her rash decision to elope the previous summer. Only a sudden inclination on Darcy's part sent him to Ramsgate in time to see his sister saved from the worst mistake of her young life. At fifteen years of age, Georgiana had no idea of the world's evils, one of whom was George Wickham, the scoundrel who sought Georgiana's hefty dowry and revenge against Darcy. Arriving at Ramsgate to see his only sibling handed into a rented hack by the rake, it took the sum of Darcy's control not to shoot the man on sight. Richard would have drawn his sword, not allowing Wickham another breath.

The failed elopement, if known, would have been a blight on the Darcy name, something he could, or rather, would not allow. Darcy easily imagined Gerald Darcy's response had he known his son's failure, for there was no doubt in Darcy's mind who was at fault. If he had heard it once, he heard it a thousand times; the Darcy name was a sacred trust to hold above all others. The Ramsgate incident was the only time the son was grateful that his father was gone.

Three months later, his sister, raised by the same stern parent, continued to wallow in her insistence on penance and forgiveness. She cried at the slightest edge to Darcy's tone. She sobbed even if the matter upsetting him had nothing to do with her. Darcy was at his wit's end. With Richard leaving…

"You are thinking of Ramsgate, are you not?" his cousin asked.

"How can I not? I chose to send her there. I hired her villainous companion. I never explained to Georgiana that some men are treacherous. I rented a beachfront house so she would have access to stunning views. No good came from her being close to the ocean. I knew better!" Darcy huffed. "Is it happenstance that she was harmed near the sea? No, Richard. Our grandmother lost her life when her carriage turned over into a rain-filled ditch. My mother…*blast!* I cannot imagine what she would say if she knew her only son placed her beloved Georgie so close to the water. Who else should I blame?"

"Your reasoning is not sound. This will be my third trip to the continent. The other two sailing journeys were entirely uneventful. It is not the water's fault." Richard shook his head. "Accidents happen, Darcy. As a soldier, I know this more than most. You must release this fear, or it will eat you alive."

Gritting his teeth until his cheeks hurt, Darcy changed

the subject. "God be with you, Richard. I have heard the reports from Spain. You will be fighting against a very determined Napoleon. How long will you be away?"

His cousin rubbed his hands together. "I have trained. My regiment is well-equipped and prepared. We shall end this war and be done with this chaos, Darcy, or I will die trying."

"Do not *ever* utter those words in my hearing, Richard. I cannot"—he inhaled sharply—"I will not question your honor or valor by suggesting that you shirk a duty to which you have sworn, but your life is worth more to me than the land, the power, or the coffers our rulers covet."

Richard dipped his head a fraction, acknowledging Darcy's emotions.

"Will your father not use his influence to keep you from the front lines?"

The colonel scoffed. "You should know by now that the vainglorious Lord Matlock would never trouble himself for his children when his greatest joy is inflicting misery upon the poor souls who unwisely 'borrow' from him and his rotten-hearted business associates. It's a foul game he plays with the lives of the desperate."

"I find it hard to believe how easily he is able to fool others."

"Do not forget, Darcy, that Father has a partner in Sir Leigh Barrett, the most renowned expert in European and Egyptian antiquities in the land. With Sir Barrett's so-called expert appraisals, miserable men looking to invest are taken in. Additionally, would you not agree that it is the desire of the wealthy to display all the rarities their money can buy in their great houses? Why, Uncle Gerald filled the tables and shelves of Pemberley with priceless treasures from the ancient past."

"You are correct. My father enjoyed the hunt, particularly for rare maps. When he discovered one he was able to purchase, he rejoiced. When a map was offered that proved to be fake, he was angry for days."

"At least your father was honest with his approach. Mine used a crook dressed as a gentleman fallen on hard times to offer his artifacts for sale. The victim believes he is getting a steal. The truth is that he is being stolen from."

"Who is his latest prey?"

"Some poor sod from Cornwall who desires nothing more than to supplement his daughter's dowry. Father offered him a statue with an 'indisputable' provenance for the cost of the pittance already set aside for his child. As usual, the gentleman will learn of the deceit only after he stirs himself to offer his unknown fake artifact to the highest bidder. By then, the girl's portion will be tucked away in one of Father's bulging accounts where the money and my father are untouchable."

"Why does no one step forward? Surely, if enough of his victims made claims against him, then justice might be meted out." Darcy's sense of honor was stirred.

"Against Lord Matlock, the ruling voice of the House of Lords and close personal friend of the Prince Regent?" Richard mocked. "Since much of these ill-gotten gains pads the pockets of said prince, nothing will be done even if all those affected were to unite."

Darcy knew Richard's comments to be true. His uncle loaned money to impoverished gentlemen and then pressured them to support his political causes, along with paying exorbitant interest on the debt. Occasionally, he dabbled with counterfeit historical finds that somehow happened to come into his hands, selling them for an outrageous profit. Hugh Fitzwilliam was the epitome of greed. His eldest son, Frederick, Viscount Smithton, was almost a twin in avarice. His only distinction from his father besides age was his lack of cunning. Men like them stirred the cauldron against

Napoleon because war meant increased business in the armaments trade, of which his uncle was a partner.

"What of your brother? Would he come to your assistance?"

Richard snorted. "Freddy is an imbecile. He was so drunk recently that he approached Lady Eleanor Witherspoon at a crowded theater and offered her *carte blanche.* It is a wonder her husband did not shoot my brother on sight."

Darcy groaned.

Richard continued. "Besides, I am not one to run to someone else for help. I have chosen my path and am content."

"Then, is there anything within my power to ease your way? What of funds? Do you need a new pistol or blade? Come, Richard. Allow me to help you in some way."

His cousin cleared his throat before looking him directly in the eye. "There is something I require." Richard paused as if choosing his words carefully. "Since the loss of your father five years ago…no, since well before then, you have carried out your duty to an infinitesimal degree. In caring for so many, one thing eludes you. I want you…no, I beg you…to discover something or someone that brings you joy. Cultivate a hobby that calms you or, better yet, find a woman who delights your days and pleasures you at night, someone who fills your heart and shares your trials. Find happiness and hold onto it with a tight grip, Darcy. Once you discover its source, never let it go."

Richard had no idea what he was asking of him. "I do not…."

His cousin added his final thrust: "If you ever want Georgiana to achieve happiness, you must take the lead. From experience, you know that wealth is not the answer, nor is power. The older you get, the more like your father you become, and though he had many good qualities, he was bitter and standoffish. Find a lady who yearns to love you as much as you yearn to be loved. Then, I will have everything I need." Before he strolled from the room, he said, "I will tell Georgiana of my plans." With a salute, he was gone.

Richard was an integral part of Darcy's youth and adult life. During the prior two occasions when his cousin was fighting in France, Darcy scoured the papers and made himself a pest at the war office for news. Each time Richard returned, battle-hardened but alive, Darcy could finally breathe again.

He sank into a chair. Closing his eyes, reminiscing, one image after another flashed across his mind until his world seemed to spin.

When Darcy was eight or nine, Richard, two years older, challenged him to a cow milking contest. Both boys spent part of the year on their family's sizeable estates. The rest of their time was spent either with their tutors or in London. Neither had ever milked a cow. Darcy was in the lead by a few drops when his cow shifted her weight, catching her hoof atop the bucket. He could not move fast enough to save any of the precious liquid. Richard guffawed until his cow took exception to his humor and kicked his bucket too. Darcy laughed so hard that he fell backward off the stool. As usual, their competition ended in a tie.

Darcy recalled the day at Eton when he received the letter trimmed in black. Lady Anne had been Darcy's confidant, his fortress where he could relax and find peace when the demands of the father were too much for the son. The loss of such a wonderful woman left him floundering. Richard made sure Darcy ate and that he left the hushed quiet of his room. It was Richard who protected him when older boys taunted him. Richard gave him purpose when his father would not allow him to return home for the funeral.

The day of his father's burial flashed across Darcy's mind.

Lord Matlock demanded the rights to the Darcy ancestral estates and access to all of Darcy's investments. His aunt Lady Catherine de Bourgh, Lord Matlock's older sister, insisted that the newly appointed master of Pemberley marry her only daughter to allow Lady Catherine the freedom to spend those same assets. Only Richard stood at Darcy's side until Darcy could stand on his own. Richard showed Lord Matlock and Lady Catherine de Bourgh the door, comforted Georgiana, and set the servants to tasks establishing Darcy as the sole master.

Darcy rubbed his chest. So much had happened in his lifetime. It was as if Shakespeare had written a three-act tragedy set at Pemberley. Men like his cousin were rare. Darcy held him in deep respect. Yet, in truth, Richard had to be wrong. He found pleasure in many things, did he not?

Resting his head on the back of his chair, Darcy considered his routine and that of his sister. Since her near elopement, she appeared to traverse each day by rote. He passed the time by investigating one business venture after another, giving his hours purpose.

Darcy growled. Richard was correct. His sister was not happy, and neither was he.

He stood, calling for his butler. Before Richard's arrival, he intended to journey to Hertfordshire and help his friend Charles Bingley settle into first-time management of a large property. Darcy would not stay the full two months as he had initially accepted. Instead, he would help Bingley, return to London, take up a hobby, and find the woman of his dreams.

Bah! Although he admired Richard's intelligence and courage, try as he might, finding a woman of his exacting expectations was unlikely.

* * *

Five hours later, he had installed Georgiana with Lady Matlock at Matlock House. Darcy was approaching Bingley's leased estate, Netherfield Park. Hertfordshire's location offered quick access to London, a journey needing only one stop. His town coach traversed the roads with ease, allowing him to read the latest prospectus from his man of business. He occasionally glanced out the window at the harvested fields, the rows barren except for the tell-tale traces of the wheat's stalks. One farm looked much like the next.

A narrow river ran the length of the roadway, the water running quickly from the autumn rains. His coachman knew to stay on the far side of the road.

At last, the road curved to the south, providing a panoramic view of the main house. It was a three-story brick edifice covered in green ivy with a white portico held up by two large Grecian columns. The door opened and out stepped Bingley.

"Welcome to Netherfield Park." Bingley rocked up on the toes of his feet, a large grin plastered across his face. Before Darcy could descend the carriage steps, his friend asked, "Did you have a good trip? Was the North Road improved? I say, we had a rough go of it yesterday. Both my sisters complained during the whole length of the journey. However, you will not need to worry about Louisa or Caroline. They are preparing to impress the locals at an assembly this evening in Meryton. I do hope you brought your dancing slippers, Darcy. You have a short time to rest before we leave. I will have a light supper served in your room."

So much for finding happiness in Hertfordshire! Richard would be thrilled he would attend a public assembly. Darcy despised dancing with strangers.

Darcy opened his mouth to beg off from the assembly when Bingley continued. "Say, what do you think of the house? It is rather grand looking if I might say so myself.

Several of the neighbors happened by to welcome us to the area. Both Louisa and her husband seem satisfied with our arrangement. I fear Caroline will wait for you to express your opinion before she tells me what she thinks. If you like it, then so will she. If you do not, I fear she will be unbearable."

He ached to shout that Miss Caroline Bingley was already unbearable. Instead, Darcy gritted his teeth, feigned a smile, and followed his host within.

* * *

Darcy tugged at his sleeves. That Bingley had insisted they attend the assembly after he had traveled for half of the day was the mark of a thoughtless host. It reminded him how young and inexperienced was his friend. Bingley did not feel confident enough to enter a room full of his neighbors alone. Nevertheless, ill-start or no, Bingley's amiable character would soon have him making friends. Darcy, on the other hand, would meet no one of importance.

The small town came into view, the roadway lit by lanterns and the glow of a moon that would reach its zenith the following night. People spilled from the local inn. From inside Bingley's carriage, they could hear music playing through an open window on the first floor.

Miss Bingley groaned. "Charles, I cannot imagine why you would believe that any of us would want to spend time with farmers and their wives. Why, they will stare at us, examining every inch of our clothing and hair. I cannot help but think they will attempt to put themselves forward to Louisa and me." She leant toward Darcy. "Certainly, Mr. Darcy would not have come had you not insisted."

Even though she was correct, he chose not to agree with her. Caroline Bingley was a grasping, ambitious female with little care who she stepped on to gain access to the highest circles of society. To her, Darcy was nothing more than a ticket to enter his sphere of elevated rank.

Never!

Clearing his throat, he said, "Bingley, at the first opportunity, do not be surprised if I call for the carriage and return to Netherfield. I am weary and not fit for company."

"I will go with you, Mr. Darcy." Miss Bingley slid closer on the bench seat. "We can spend the rest of the evening in quiet repose."

"Caroline!" Bingley and his eldest sister, Louisa Hurst, exclaimed.

She waved her hand at them. "Nonsense, Darcy knows what I mean." She tilted her head toward him, her eyelashes fluttering.

He could see the longing in her expression but held no compunction about crushing it. "I am not fit for company, Miss Bingley. Therefore, I shall return alone." He muttered, "Let us be done with this."

Descending from the carriage, the crowd parted, allowing Bingley's party to step inside the room. Within seconds, Darcy heard speculation of his and Bingley's annual income and marital prospects passed from one person to the next. Miss Bingley erred. The women were not surveying the fabric and design of her clothing and coiffure. Instead, their avaricious eyes were looking straight at him.

Those already inside the building were a motley group from every level of local society. Unlike his home shire, where he was well known, these were strangers. He wanted to pull at his collar, reclaim his coat, and leave. Instead, his chin thrust upwards as his eyes surveyed the room. From experience, Darcy knew the chill of his gaze would keep even the boldest away. Only the foolish would approach.

CHAPTER 3

*E*lizabeth Bennet's toe tapped in time to the lively tune. She danced the first two sets with Robbie and then John Lucas. Their enthusiasm far exceeded their skill. Thus, she was grateful neither asked for the third. Jane barely avoided Bertie Lucas by dancing the first and second with their uncle Phillips. Mary read a book in the corner while Kitty and Lydia danced with each other. Good partners were scarce in Meryton.

Despite this, the dance floor was crowded. Those unfortunate enough not to have a partner filled the chairs set along the walls. Elizabeth stood with her eldest sister Jane where they had a clear view of the five individuals who entered the room.

The sight of a new party signaled the dancers to stop and stare. Having anyone outside their small community attend their local assembly was highly unusual. Therefore, the newcomers captured the attention of every gossiping matron, grasping mother, and unattached girl in the building.

Like her neighbors, Elizabeth studied the newcomers.

The first to enter was an amiable sort with an inviting grin. He was probably in his early to mid-twenties with blondish hair, average height, and wearing a fashionable rose-colored waistcoat that matched the ribbon on Jane's gown. He was gifted with a dimple on each cheek.

Jane's sigh caught Elizabeth's attention. Her sister's gaze focused on the young man. Arching her brow, Elizabeth suspected the evening might be interesting after all.

To his right was a slightly older couple whose intentions were less certain. Brushing the woman's hand from his arm, the heavy-set, balding man set out for the drinks table. The lady pouted. *Married!*

Next, Elizabeth's eyes fixed upon the man at the back. He was undeniably handsome with a tall and imposing figure. *Was he skilled on the dance floor, or would his long legs and broad shoulders wreak havoc on those already standing up for a set?* Elizabeth hoped to find out.

Glancing to his right, Elizabeth's hopes for a reel dashed to the ground. A lovely woman with perfectly braided and curled hair, bright eyes, high cheekbones, a straight nose, and full lips appeared glued to his side. Dressed to perfection, she could only be described as *lovely*. From the way her slender hand wrapped around the gentleman's arm, she was his. Or he was hers. Either way, they were attached. *Well, drat!*

Before the party from Netherfield arrived, there had been much speculation about the number of Mr. Bingley's guests. To her mother's frustration, Mr. Thomas Bennet, her husband of twenty-five years, had not roused himself from his bookroom to greet their newest neighbor, gleaning no information like the other fathers with unmarried daughters had done. Reports of twelve men and three ladies residing at the estate were grossly exaggerated for, unless others remained behind, the five entering the room completed the party. Only the smiling man standing before them was the lone available target for Meryton's matchmaking mothers, Elizabeth's included.

"Jane, Lizzy, Mary, Kitty, Lydia! Come! We must welcome our new neighbors." Mrs. Francine Bennet, who had used her youthful vivacity to capture a husband, pushed her most beautiful daughter, Jane, to the forefront. Lydia then Kitty were next. Since Mary refused to budge from her post next to the wall, Elizabeth brought up the rear.

Sir William Lucas performed the brief introduction.

Mr. Bingley bowed. "It is my pleasure." His eyes flashed to Jane and held fast. "My family and guest are pleased to make your acquaintance. My sister, Mrs. Louisa Hurst, and her husband, Mr. Hurst." He gestured somewhere behind him. "My other sister, Miss Caroline Bingley, and my good friend, Fitzwilliam Darcy from Derbyshire and London, are delighted with Meryton. Have you lived here long?" He barely hesitated before adding, "Miss Bennet, if I might have the honor of your next available set?"

A tale-tell blush rose from Jane's neck to her cheeks. "It would be my pleasure."

Elizabeth's eyes darted between the two. Both Mr. Bingley and Jane grinned broadly. That Jane, reticent even in private, would show her happiness upon so brief an introduction indicated her interest more than any words could have done.

As Mr. Bingley led her sister to the dance floor, their mother crowed her triumph to the room. "I knew how it would be as soon as Mr. Bingley set his eyes upon my Jane."

Elizabeth was mortified. If Jane had not been fully engaged in conversation with the gentleman, she would have rushed from the building to hide away at Longbourn. Would her mother ever learn? Elizabeth doubted it.

Peeking at Mr. Darcy and Miss Bingley to ascertain their reaction to Francine Bennet's boasts, Elizabeth was unsurprised at the disgust radiating from their expressions. Even though they were not married as she had initially guessed, they looked like a matched pair. *Boorish!*

Inherently, Elizabeth knew neither would condescend to think kindly on any of the Bennets nor the rest of the neighborhood. *Well, who were they to her?* Deciding that the best course was to modify her family's behavior, Elizabeth would spend the remainder of the evening tempering her mother's expressions of conquest and the liveliness of her younger sisters so no more reproach could be stacked upon their reputations. It would not do for Mr. Bingley's guest or sister to judge Jane Bennet as unworthy based on the actions of others.

Before the music started for the next set, Elizabeth encouraged her younger sisters to search for a partner. Mary had not looked away from the pages of *Fordyce's Sermons.*

With her sisters engaged and her mother whispering gossip with Lady Lucas, Elizabeth was free to enjoy the fruits of her efforts. Standing at the edge of the room, she observed the couples as they moved gracefully to the music. Despite the lack of skill on the part of some, the joy on their faces warmed Elizabeth's heart, especially that of Mr. Bingley and Jane. They were a lovely pair.

As the dancers swirled around the room, gossip about the newcomers abounded. Mrs. Long loudly declared, "It is rumored that Mr. Darcy has a grand estate that rivals Chatsworth in the Derbyshire hills. He also is reported to have a house in a fashionable area of London. All he needs is a wife to run his homes."

Mrs. Goulding replied, "Well, that is nothing. I heard that the gentleman's annual income is in excess of ten thousand pounds." She chortled. "A wife would have a grand time spending all that money, I have no doubt."

Mrs. Long offered her rebuttal. "Mr. Bingley's five thousand a year pales compared to Mr. Darcy. I must admit that the gentleman from Derbyshire's fine, tall person, handsome features, and noble mien first captured my eye."

Mrs. Goulding agreed vigorously; the lone feather in her hair bobbed up and down, reminding Elizabeth of a chicken.

Mrs. Long continued. "However, his propensity to ignore and refusal to dance with any ladies has changed my opinion. Mr. Bingley's easy, unaffected manners render him a far better catch. I hope that if he quits looking at Jane Bennet, he might focus on my Minerva. She is older than Jane by three weeks and has a more sizable portion."

Mrs. Goulding scoffed. "My two nieces are also worthy of Mr. Bingley's attention. Perhaps he will look their way instead. Although with Mr. Darcy's wealth, my nieces could overlook his surly mien. Independence could be purchased by the wife of a rich man."

Their attitudes unsettled Elizabeth. She crossed the room before the two ladies fell into their typical argument of whose progeny were more desirable on the marriage mart. If truth be told, once Mr. Bingley saw Jane, he would likely look at no other.

When the music ended, Mr. Bingley kindly returned Jane to her mother before joining Mr. Darcy.

"Come, Darcy," Mr. Bingley said, "I must have you dance. I hate to see you standing about by yourself in this stupid manner. You had much better dance."

Mr. Darcy crossed his arms over his chest. "I certainly shall not. You know how I detest it unless I am particularly acquainted with the lady. At an assembly such as this, it would be insupportable. There is not a woman in the room with whom it would not be a punishment for me to partner."

"I would not be so fastidious as you are for a kingdom!" cried Mr. Bingley, revealing the warmth of his personality. "Upon my honor, I never met with so many pleasant girls in my life as I have this evening; and there are several of them, you see, who are uncommonly pretty."

"*You* are dancing with the only handsome girl in the room." The taller man sneered, looking at Jane.

Elizabeth held her breath, all anticipation of Mr. Bingley's response. She was not disappointed.

"Oh, she is the most beautiful creature I ever beheld! But there is one of her sisters standing just behind you, who is very pretty, and, I dare say, very agreeable. Do let me ask my partner to introduce you to her."

Uh-oh! Mr. Bingley was looking directly at Elizabeth. *No! No! No!* She had no desire to stand up with Mr. Darcy, for he was proud, above his company, and above being pleased. All his estate in Derbyshire or the gold in his accounts could not save him from having a most forbidding, disagreeable countenance. She had no desire to dance with him.

"Which do you mean?" Turning around, he looked for a moment at Elizabeth till, catching her eye, he withdrew his own and coldly said, "She is tolerable but not handsome enough to tempt *me*, and I am in no humor at present to give consequence to young ladies who are slighted by other men. You had better return to your partner and enjoy her smiles, for you are wasting your time with me."

Elizabeth barely kept herself from gasping aloud. *What a rude man!* Never had she been publicly insulted. Her ire threatened to flood her good sense. Choosing to exercise her genteel training in comportment, she caught his eye and dipped her head to acknowledge his verbal blow without lowering her gaze from his. He may be ungentlemanly, but she was a lady.

* * *

The air was heavy with smoke from a hundred candles lighting the room. The smell of sweaty and perfumed bodies jostling against each other on the small dance floor only increased Darcy's discomfort. He should never have come. Bingley pressing him to dance with an unknown girl of questionable background was, according to the ancient Arab proverb, the final straw.

He barked at a passing attendant to have Bingley's carriage brought around. Darcy desperately needed privacy and silence. Taking a last look at the lady Bingley had tried to pair him with, his eyes met hers, and she tilted her head saucily. Instead of humility and acceptance of his superior rank, he was struck by her attitude. Her eyes sparkled in the candlelight as one brow arched.

Good lord! He needed to get out of there. Turning away from the brazen chit who could not even recognize an insult when she heard one, Darcy draped his great coat across his shoulders, grabbed his walking stick, gloves, and hat, and departed the building.

A gust of October wind lifted his collar as the squeak of rusty hinges drew his attention to the inn's sign swaying above him—the *White Stag.* There were inns with the same name all over England. Why he must have passed a dozen of them… Darcy looked from the portico to the road, where he had a view of the businesses on the side of the street, stepping into a scene from his past.

Was he in his fourteenth year when his father detoured from the North Road to this same small town? No, he was only thirteen since that was his first year at Eton. Georgiana and her nurse went inside the inn, and he…Darcy rubbed his chin. He had walked toward a bridge. *Was he in the right place?* Darcy had not thought of the young sea captain for years. He racked his memory.

HMS Discovery? HMS Vantage?

He recalled two girls, sisters, if he remembered correctly. Three lads abandoned ship at the idea of missing a meal. Apple tarts, he recalled.

Ah, yes. HMS Voyager! The raft that never made it beyond the first bend. The young captain was determined, he gave her that. Memories finally began to connect. She had a map drawn from one her father possessed. Her goal was to sail to South America and discover Inca gold.

Darcy chuckled, remembering her fearless determination.

He glanced up at the windows where the candlelight flickered as swarms of people moved underneath them. Was the little captain at the assembly? She must be about one and twenty. Nay, he recalled no mischievous sailor gathering her crew when he had quickly surveyed the room upon arrival. Likely, she had gone into service or was already married with a child or two weighing her down.

More than the girl, he remembered his father's attitude when he returned to gather his family and get back on the road to Pemberley. Gerald Darcy never revealed his purpose for the detour nor whom he sought in the small village. Darcy only knew the excursion resulted in intense anger that his father had embraced for days. It was the most uncomfortable trip they had ever made in the same carriage. His father immediately rebuffed any attempts he made to gain information.

Darcy knew beyond a shadow of a doubt that his father's carriage took the right fork at the bridge. When he had arrived earlier at Netherfield Park, Darcy had crossed that same bridge, his carriage going to the left. Who or what was on that other fork?

He spied a group of grooms and drivers warming themselves around a fire. "Pardon me. I am staying at Netherfield Park. Can you tell me where the west road ends and what I might find on the way?"

One chap spoke up. "That'll be Longbourn. There be a stable and chapel in addition to the main house. The Bennets have held the property for near two hundred years, give or take a few. The father is a smart one who keeps to his self. The mother, she flits about like a moth. The girls, all five of them, be as different as ducks."

"I see." Darcy nodded his head in appreciation. Mr. Bennet of Longbourn. He was not familiar with any Bennets in his sphere. Likely Bennet was landed gentry who rarely came to Town. *Wait! Bennet?* Was that not the name of Bingley's latest interest, who had a bevy of sisters? A sick feeling stirred his gut. "Do you know the names of the daughters?"

"Surely, we all do. Miss Jane, Miss Lizzy, Miss Catherine, Miss Lydia, and there be a middle girl, but I always forget her name. Just a minute, wait…ah, yes, it be Miss Mary."

Jane and Lizzy!

The pieces of the puzzle fell into place. If Darcy was correct, the exact location where he now stood was where his father deposited him all those years ago. If he strolled to the bridge, he would overlook the very spot where he discovered the drama enacted below, that of Captain Lizzy and the *HMS Voyager*. Her blonde-haired sister, Jane, had been on the bank attempting to discourage her from sailing.

He could not believe he was able to conjure the images so clearly. Just thinking about that moment in time lightened his heart.

The years had been kind to the Bennet girls—if it was them. Jane Bennet had grown into a lovely woman. It was no wonder Bingley's eyes had settled on her and not moved. Then there was *Captain Lizzy*. He had not thought of her in over a decade. Was that her in the assembly room with the pert attitude? If so, he gravely insulted her.

He was a dunce!

CHAPTER 4

*E*lizabeth was shocked. Although Jane's beauty and countenance regularly received compliments, Elizabeth's wit and ready sense of humor were often favorably remarked upon. Never had such hateful words been spoken against her person. Haughty Mr. Darcy's insult revealed a meanness of character unknown to her.

Intolerable! What a horrible thing to say about a lady—made worse as he spoke directly to her, for the man's eyes had scanned the crowd before resting squarely upon her face. *Brute!*

Hurt vied with ire, rendering her feeling somehow less about herself. Elizabeth vowed to show him she would not be intimidated. Boldly, she tipped her head to him, smirking instead of sobbing. Elizabeth pressed her lips together, blinked quickly, then watched him walk out the door, grateful that he chose not to engage anyone else in conversation. It would not do for her neighbors to also feel the sting of his vitriol.

She was not the only person watching him leave. Miss Bingley and Mrs. Hurst loudly discussed whether they should follow their guest whilst Mr. Bingley stood with his mouth agape.

Others looked at her. Elizabeth could see the sympathy in their eyes. To be publicly cut was a blow to any lady's reputation. The wound might affect her for a lifetime if she allowed it. Tears threatened, but she would not cry.

Lifting her chin, Elizabeth chose ire over pain. Her blood boiled until it blocked the sound of the whispers following the man's departure.

"Lizzy, are you well?" Charlotte Lucas whispered as she softly touched Elizabeth's arm.

Spinning toward her longtime friend, Elizabeth swallowed her hurt and smiled. "I have never been better, for had that cur remained, I might have had to dance with him, which would have been truly 'intolerable.'"

Charlotte tilted her face to study Elizabeth closely. "Only you, dear Lizzy, could find humor amidst insult. I admire you. Come. Let us reassure the others that you are not bleeding from a mortal wound."

"Yes, dear Lottie." Elizabeth tucked her arm in the crook of her friend's elbow. "Let's ignore the cursed man and enjoy ourselves, for rarely have I had fodder for the ridiculous delivered to my person with such alacrity."

Charlotte chuckled. "Pray, tell me right away, what nonsensical name are you calling him in that brain of yours, for I have no doubt you are doing so."

"Pompous Pete was the first that came to my mind. However, his name has such a tone of arrogance to perfectly fit the fellow that I cannot but think I need to give this a bit more thought."

"Fitzwilliam Darcy? You find his name arrogant?"

"And you do not?" was Elizabeth's immediate reply. "Those of elevated rank favor epithets of at least three syllables. I would imagine his parents compiled a list of possibilities before they wed of what they would call their heir. Archibald! That's it. He will forever be Mr. Archibald Arse-y instead of Fitzwilliam Darcy when I think of him, which will be *never*."

"You are wicked, Lizzy Bennet, and I love you for it." Charlotte pulled her close to where their mothers were discussing every move and expression displayed by the Bingley party. "Do be careful, Lizzy, for I understand from Father that Mr. Darcy is connected to the most influential families in England. He has tremendous power himself. It would not do to make an enemy of him. Let him overlook you. It is the safer course."

"Charlotte Lucas! I always follow the safe course, do I not?"

Charlotte grinned. "Not always, my friend."

* * *

"Oh, look! Mr. Bingley is dancing again with my Jane." Elizabeth's mother was loud enough that her voice was certain to be heard above the music and outside the building. She and Charlotte's mother were seated close together, competing to be heard. "I have long told you how it would be, Maude. My Jane could not be so beautiful for nothing."

Lady Lucas glared at the Bennet matron. "Yes, Fanny, you have always said that of Jane. However, not all your daughters have found favor for Mr. Bingley's exalted guest took exception to Lizzy, did he not?"

Elizabeth's mother harrumphed. "At least he noticed one of *my* daughters." She must have caught movement out of the corner of her eye, for she said, "Say, can you believe Minerva Long is wearing an orange ribbon with her complexion? Why, she looks almost thirty instead of the same age as Jane. My good friend, you have a far too discerning eye ever to allow Charlotte or Maria to wear that color."

Lady Lucas, appreciating the compliment, nodded her agreement. "Not my girls. In fact, was that not the very ribbon we told the haberdasher he would be keeping for the next ten years unless he reduced the price?"

Francine Bennet tilted her head to her friend. "Maude, we both know how best to present our girls in public. Why did you know…"

Elizabeth stopped listening, as did Charlotte.

"I will never live this down, will I?" Elizabeth pouted. "I will forever be the lady Mr. Darcy considered unworthy. Well, let me tell you, Lottie, my appearance may be intolerable to him, but his character is intolerable to me."

Charlotte teased. "You would not marry him if he asked?"

Elizabeth spun to look directly at her friend. "How could you suggest such a thing? Never! I shall marry only where there is deep respect and tender affection or not marry at all. I would never become Mrs. Archibald Arse-y for all the money in the Bank of England or all the jewels belonging to the crown."

The two girls laughed until Bertie Lucas approached.

"Papa said I had to dance with you, Lottie. I guess now's as good a time as any."

Charlotte rolled her eyes at her silly younger brother.

As the siblings moved away, Elizabeth's mind stewed over the overheard insult. What sort of man would cut down a stranger with the slash of his rapier-sharp tongue? Only the vilest. Was his life so filled with self-importance that he could no longer see value in others? Surely, he would have to be miserable to be that critical.

If money and position rendered a person unkind, she would shun any attempt to improve her circumstances.

Watching Mr. Bingley hurry to the table to bring Jane a

refreshing drink, Elizabeth wondered at the friendship. If rumors were true, Mr. Bingley had not been raised a gentleman. His family was firmly rooted in trade. How in the world had someone like Fitzwilliam Darcy befriended an amiable man?

A thought hit Elizabeth directly between the eyes. She almost gasped aloud.

Why had Mr. Bingley not defended her to his friend? A gentleman would never allow another to insult a lady publicly. He should have immediately taken Mr. Darcy to task, forcing an apology at the very least.

What sort of man was Mr. Bingley? Was his friendly appearance a façade? If so, she would do anything to discern his character before he had a chance to hurt Jane. Elizabeth had no clue how she would go about it, but she would use the most efficient means possible, one that would keep her from Mr. Darcy's company.

Wishing Mr. Darcy had not arrived in Meryton, Elizabeth decided that the wisest course would be to ignore him when possible and be on her guard when it was not.

* * *

DARCY RELAXED in the quiet of Bingley's library with the happy memory of the little girl with no front teeth keeping him company. What would his life be had he the freedom to pursue his desires instead of the expectations of society and his family? He would never know.

Despite having to listen to Caroline Bingley disparage the attendees of the assembly (in particular the Bennet females) upon their return hours later, he disagreed. Although he had slighted Miss Elizabeth's appearance, upon closer recollection of the night's events, his second opinion proved that his initial comments were indeed wrong.

The former captain had grown into a lovely young woman. Her teeth came in straight and white. Her face had slimmed.

Bingley interrupted his thoughts. "By the way, Darcy…" Bingley sipped from his snifter once his sisters had retired to their rooms. The candles in the library flickered as the wicks burned low. "Your rapid departure after your harsh statements about Miss Elizabeth Bennet was much commented upon by my neighbors. I fear you did not leave the best impression."

At first, Darcy chaffed at the comment. Who were these people to him? They were his friend's neighbors, not his. Then he considered how Bingley needed all the help he could to establish himself. That he had made matters more challenging for him was intolerable. Straightening his spine, Darcy replied, "My comments were harsh and unjustified. I apologize for giving cause for dissension between you and your neighbors." At Bingley's nod, he continued. "I assume you explained that I was tired from my travels and was unaware of the assembly before I arrived. That should have softened their hurt feelings, I suppose."

Bingley's jaw dropped. "I did not think of it. In truth, my sole aim was to dance again with Miss Bennet."

Darcy's fingers tightened around the arm of the chair. "I see." A gentleman never insulted a lady—ever. The words he uttered against the young woman rose in Darcy's gut until bitterness lingered at the back of his throat.

Since there had not been an introduction to Mr. Bennet, he was likely not in attendance. Therefore, Miss Elizabeth had no protector.

It was good that Darcy knew she was fierce; at least, she was as a child.

"I should have said something." Bingley rubbed his hands over his face. "Miss Bennet claims Miss Elizabeth as her closest sister. She praised her diligence in educating herself and her younger sisters. There are five girls, you know."

Darcy nodded.

"Their estate is entailed." Bingley waved his hand in the air. "Oh, Miss Bennet did not share that information, but those in attendance were happy to speak of the Bennet family. According to Mr. Long, due to indifferent parenting, their portions are trifling, so the ladies will need all the help they can muster to make a good match. Because of the number of eligible men currently fighting France, the odds of an unmarried woman finding a worthy mate is small. Little may be gained from their efforts, despite their beauty and charm."

"It is the same throughout England," Darcy noted. "This makes the targets on our backs exponentially larger."

"I suspect that Cupid's arrow has already pierced my heart." Bingley rubbed his chest.

"Be cautious, my friend. Many lovely ladies are encouraged to show more affection than they feel to increase their family's security. You would not be the first nor the last to discover after she signed the parish registry as Mrs. Bingley that you married a harpy with a grasping family in tow."

Bingley set his glass aside. "Be that as it may, I believe I could search all of Britain and not find as gentle a soul as Jane Bennet. I offer you a good night, for I yearn to see her dance across my dreams."

Darcy emptied the snifter. The Bible claimed that the tongue could cause tremendous damage if let loose. *But the tongue can no man tame; it is an unruly evil, full of deadly poison.* He wished he would have tamed his speech. Had someone told Georgiana she was intolerable or not handsome enough, Darcy would have cut out the cur's appendage from his treacherous mouth.

Blast! He owed Miss Elizabeth an apology.

Darcy knew he was far from perfect. Nonetheless, he strove to live up to the highest standards. From birth, he understood that any man who would take out his frustrations on an innocent female was bereft of honor.

Good lord! What a horrible entry into Hertfordshire. He was worse than a dunce. His parents would have been deeply ashamed of his conduct. He was deeply ashamed too.

* * *

HIS VALET ENTERED HIS CHAMBERS. "Sir, if you plan to venture out of doors, you should know that the weather has become quite brisk." Parker held up a woolen waistcoat in each hand.

Throwing back the quilt, Darcy shivered and gestured to the light gray instead of the red. Brushing the heavy curtains aside, he peered out on a world encrusted with white. The light frost glistened in the sun, appearing to give life to the dying vegetation. Like the year before, hints of early winter shimmered across the countryside.

"Send word to ready my horse. I will ride after I break my fast."

"Very good, sir."

Less than an hour later, Darcy, Bingley, and Hurst galloped alongside the same harvested fields he observed the day prior. The ground was well-packed with very few ruts despite recent rains.

Bingley slowed his mount to a walk. "According to my steward, Mr. Morris, the harvest did not go well, and the revenue was down." He stood up in his stirrups, shading his eyes with his hand. "He is reputed to be a good and honest man. Yet, when I look at the rich color of the soil and the number of stalks at the sides of these fields, I cannot imagine why more was not produced. The accounting books show that even the rents collected this year are less than those of three years ago."

Darcy nodded, proud of his friend for his interest in the land. "Too much rain during the summer months." Darcy dismounted at the edge of the field. Knowing he would face Parker's disapproval later, his boot sank to well above his ankle. The slurping sound lifting his Hessian from the mire revealed how much water remained. "If you recall, during 1810, there were weeks of flooding. When it was not raining, the air was thick with damp fog. Likewise, we have had colder spring and summer months this year. I would guess your steward harvested the grain earlier than other landowners who were far less cautious. Pemberley's crops and rents suffered as well."

"Oh, I am happy to know I am not alone then." Bingley grinned. "We were in London in January when the Thames froze and in May when thunderstorms struck nine days in a row. I never considered how the weather would affect the farms. It was most uncomfortable to try to be visible in society when everyone was, as they say in Scotland, 'hunkered down.'"

Hurst added, "I was ready to take my chances with the lightning with all the screaming Caroline and Louisa did with every thunderclap. It fairly drove me to drink." He guffawed at his own joke.

Darcy knew Hurst's reputation well. His was an unhappy marriage. He needed Louisa Bingley's twenty thousand, and she craved advancing her status by marrying a distant cousin of a baronet. Hurst liked his drink long before he wed.

Because of marriages like Mr. and Mrs. Hurst, Darcy was in no hurry to attach himself to any female. His aunt, Lady Catherine de Bourgh, insisted he marry her only child, who was in no position to be the proper mistress of a grand estate. Anne de Bourgh was sickly and petulant. He shuddered at the thought of.... There would be no coupling between him and Anne. Ever!

His other aunt, Helen Fitzwilliam, Lady Matlock, interfered by hunting down the most advantageous partners for Darcy, those whose families had deep roots in the aristocracy. It mattered not if the lady was knowledgeable or kind. Pedigree was the key, according to Aunt Helen. Unfortunately, Darcy's father had felt much the same. After all, if he, a gentleman farmer, could marry the daughter of an earl, then his son should do no less.

Gratefully, Bingley interrupted his introspection. "Longbourn is about three miles from here. Should we not visit to see that they made it home safely from the assembly? It would be neighborly of us, right?"

Hurst replied before Darcy could formulate his response. "It's that eldest girl you fancy, isn't it, Bingley? She's the latest angel who's caught your eye. Miss Bennet? Yes, I can see your eagerness to be in her company again. She seemed a good sort, not too brash like the last one you chased. Well, Darcy, what do you think? Is it true love after two dances and a spot of whispered conversation?"

"Absolutely not." From experience, Darcy knew Bingley would ignore any suggestion that he should slowly approach matters of the heart. His friend was a good man whose empathy and eye for beauty often got him into trouble. "Do you recall Miss Abercrombie? Was not her name also Jane? After one evening, you declared to any who would listen that she was the lady for you. Yet, the very next ball, you changed your mind when Mildred Brock appeared at the top of the steps with her blonde curls, blue eyes, and her—"

"And her well-filled bodice," Hurst exclaimed.

"Men!" Bingley scoffed. "Gentlemen do not notice—"

"Oh yes, they do," Hurst grunted. "You are not without

eyes. I say that even Darcy, as honorable as he is, is not blind to a woman's 'assets.'"

Pursing his lips, Darcy shook his head. The conversation had gone off track. Although he needed to see Miss Elizabeth and make reparations for his words, he was in no hurry to do so that morning. "You may journey to Longbourn if you would like. However, I intend to ride the boundaries of your property and then go to the bookshop to survey the shelves. Perhaps I will discover a treasure."

"Boundaries and books?" Hurst snorted. "It is too cold for me. I am for returning to Netherfield Park, where I shall sit in front of a warm fire with my slippers warming my toes and a glass of brandy in each hand. *That* is how real gentlemen spend these cold days." At that, Hurst turned his horse back the way they had come.

Darcy suspected Bingley would push for Longbourn. However, Bingley surprised him.

"I will join you in riding the fences and to the bookshop." Bingley waited until Darcy remounted. "I need to start filling the shelves of my empty library. Perhaps you could recommend…." He kicked his horse into a run and yelled over his shoulder. "Race you there!"

There was nothing Darcy loved more than a challenge. His horse was up to the task, as was he. Leaning over the mare's neck, they quickly caught up and passed Bingley. He thrust his fist into the air. Darcy's were bred to win.

Over the next hours, as they rode the boundaries of the fields, Bingley made several more attempts to best him. Without exception, he failed. Their last race was toward Meryton. Slowing at the edge of town, they walked their horses to the bookshop in time to see Miss Bennet and Miss Elizabeth enter the building.

CHAPTER 5

Could this morning be any more dreadful?

Mr. Bingley's attendance on Jane created eager anticipation in the maternal breast of Francine Bennet. Waking early, their mother interrupted Jane and Elizabeth's review of the assembly over their tea and toast.

"Come, you must ready yourself for the day, for I do not doubt Mr. Bingley will arrive early."

Jane asked, "Mama, are you certain he will come? Did you offer an invitation?"

"Pshaw!" Their mother waved her hand. "An invitation… why, I have never heard of such nonsense. No, he will be here. You mark my words."

"And Lizzy, you keep a tight rein on your impertinent tongue. Wealthy men disapprove of an opinionated female. They want wives of good breeding and even temper. I will not have you ruin Jane's chances with Mr. Bingley." Before they left the breakfast room, their mother added, "Jane, you must change into your pale pink gown. It highlights the glow of your cheeks. Lizzy, you…well, do something with your hair. You already have curls coming loose."

Elizabeth whispered to her sister as they ascended the stairs to their chambers, "I am terribly sorry, Miss Bennet, but I cannot offer you my hand in marriage since your favorite sister has dreadful hair."

Jane snickered. "Lizzy, I am sure that is not what Mama meant."

Jane's blind acceptance of others' faults was only good to a point. Sometimes a person needed to bear an account for unsavory or impolite actions. Not that Elizabeth viewed everyone with skepticism, or she did not believe in her heart that she did, for she found much good in people in general. She would leave cynicism to the likes of Mr. Darcy and Miss Bingley. Their view of the world from such lofty heights was obviously jaded. How horrid to miss the little daily joys that filled the lives of others. Elizabeth loved to laugh.

Three hours later, Longbourn's drawing room remained empty of male guests. Mr. Bingley had not attempted to sweep Francine Bennet's eldest daughter off her feet in a race to the altar. According to their mother, it might have been Elizabeth's unruly hair or tongue that had kept him from proposing. Although Jane was disappointed, Elizabeth was not. She was concerned that Mr. Bingley's character was not what a gentleman's should be. That he associated with Mr. Darcy did not help his cause. Just thinking of Mr. Darcy stirred her ire, so from then on, she refused to think of him at all.

Under their mother's disappointed hopes, it was preferable to escape the house. Along with their younger sisters, Jane and Elizabeth strolled to Meryton.

* * *

Soon as he stepped into the building, the quiet of Mr. Dale's store enveloped Darcy, as did the familiar scent of new and old books. Bingley rushed to Miss Bennet, who looked at the latest fashion magazines. Darcy spotted Miss Elizabeth perusing the shelves at the back of the room and joined her.

Gratefully, no one else was at that end of the store, so his apology would be private. Having recited his regrets throughout the night, he hoped she would listen. He was anxious, eager to get this behind him as he would much prefer to remind her that they had met on a prior occasion.

When he noted where her interest rested, his prepared statement vanished. "You read Voltaire?" he asked as her fingers brushed over a recently translated copy of *Candide, ou l'Optimisme*.

Her hand shot to her chest. "Mr. Darcy!"

"I beg your pardon. I had not intended to startle you." He bowed.

"An apology for startling me? Or maybe you are only building up to make reparations for your unfortunate slight on my person last evening?"

Her response, paired with the fire in her eyes, left him suddenly without words. William Congreve had been correct when he penned *The Mourning Bride* over a century prior. *Heaven has no rage like love to hatred turned. Nor Hell a fury like a woman scorned.*

"You do not need to reply, Mr. Darcy. My mother admonishes me quite regularly to guard my impertinent tongue. On this day, I have managed to control it until now. I am afraid you are the target of my failed restraint."

How had things gone awry? He was to utter his apology, and she would accept his humble admission. *Frustrating female!* Yet, he could not allow the opportunity to pass. Hurriedly, he said, "Pray, do not distress yourself, for I am indebted to you, Miss Elizabeth. My comments last evening were gauche, untrue, and unkind. Thus, I beg your forgiveness."

Her eyes pierced his. "I suspect it goes against your nature to beg for anything, sir. Nevertheless, I am not one to hold onto a grudge for long. With that said, I find I am not yet ready to let go of this one. If you do not mind, I will inform you that I vowed last night to hate you forever." She smirked, then grinned. "Your apology has purchased you some time. Knowing myself better than anyone else knows me, including my sister, Jane, I suppose I will forgive you and forget your offense within the next dozen years or so."

He chuckled, surprised at the honesty of her response. Had he been in company with the females of his circles long enough that he had become immune to the true nature of a woman? His world was pretense and pomp. Miss Elizabeth Bennet was unlike the ladies of his acquaintance.

"Miss Elizabeth, I will gladly offer penance for as long as it takes."

It was her turn to snicker. The sound was merry, a brief respite from the burdens weighing on his shoulders.

"You should be aware that I am fully capable of taking advantage of such generosity." Shifting her eyes to the book she held, she said, "To answer your initial question, Mr. Darcy, yes, I have read Voltaire. Although I do not agree entirely with his satirical impressions of the philosophy of Leibnitz, I found some truths that I hold dear."

"Did you?" He pondered her explanation. "You are not a cynic."

"Do you view yourself as one? Do you train at the same ascetic school as Antisthenes did at the feet of Socrates? Do you hold onto the tenet that virtue, rather than pleasure, is the only good and that this same quality can only be attained through rigorous self-control?"

"My sister and my estate would suffer if I did not exercise self-control. It is not a fault."

"Ah, I see. Then you hold with the current definition of a

cynic by finding fault with everyone and believe that selfishness determines the pinnacle of human behavior?"

"I am no dog." *Who was this impertinent miss? Would she even know to what or whom he referred?*

"I understand your reference. No, Mr. Darcy, you are not a dog, or you would have no fine carriage, great house, or polished boots. Diogenes, the most famous of all Antisthenes' students, was titled 'the dog' because of the choices he made to live in the public spaces of Athens, going barefoot in the snow to inure himself to the cold, all the while castigating the Athenians for their addiction to worthless luxuries. Had you been, you would have growled at me and showed your teeth."

By the end of her comment, the revelation hit him that the conversation stirred him. Instead of irritation or indifference, the ennui he experienced conversing with debutantes had vanished to be replaced by eager anticipation of her next uttered word.

He could not keep from asking, "You enjoy a debate?"

Her peal of laughter rang in his ears, then plunged to the depths of his heart. "I applaud you for referring to our animated conversation as a debate, not an argument, Mr. Darcy. I fear that only intelligent souls know the difference. And, yes, it is one of my particular delights."

He nodded, pleased with her answer. "Then might you recommend a book from the shelves since our thinking and opinions align?"

"Align? You are a confident man to make such a claim, sir."

Without hesitation, she passed two aisles and plucked Mary Wollstonecraft's *A Vindication of the Rights of Women* from the bottom shelf.

He wanted to laugh aloud. *What a woman!* Darcy stopped himself. He was thinking teasing thoughts, but he was not teasing; he never did. The desire to continue this course was tempting. A whiff of danger filled his senses. *What was he doing?* Had it been too long since he had enjoyed the company of a female? Had he ever enjoyed the company of a lady where he did not guard his comments? No, he feared he had not.

* * *

W*HAT WAS* M*R.* D*ARCY ABOUT?* His apology was unexpected. Perhaps he was not nearly as bad as she thought.

From the corner of her eye, Elizabeth's attention was grabbed, through the window at the back of the room, by two very young lads trying to catch a stray dog that had no desire to be captured. The dog's low growl and bared teeth should have warned the boys. Instead, one of them, slightly taller than the other, had his hand stretched toward the mongrel, his small fingers wiggling.

Elizabeth's heart was in her throat. "Pardon me." Shoving the book at Mr. Darcy, she ran out the door.

"Back away slowly, please." With terror, Elizabeth noted the hair standing along the ridge of the dog's spine. "Please, move away."

"But I wanna be his friend. Uncle Ralph told me I could have a dog someday an' it's as good a day as any, I s'pect." The one with the wiggling fingers spoke as the other stepped behind him.

"Oh, dear," she whispered. Elizabeth approached charily. Taking a small parcel from her reticule, she tossed a handful of its contents behind where the dog crouched. Whether it was the smell of orange coated in sticky honey or the sweet-meats dropping behind him, the dog abandoned his contention with the lads, grabbed the treat between its teeth, and ran as fast as his legs could carry him.

"But …" The boy's lower lip quivered. "We lost us a good dog, and you lost your candy."

His accent was unfamiliar to her. "You are not from the area, are you?" Running her gloved hands down his arms as she knelt, she asked, "Where are your coats? And where are your shoes?"

The skin of his arms was freezing. Elizabeth ached to take them to Longbourn to warm and feed them.

His right shoulder rose and fell, his eyes dropping to where his toe drew patterns in the dirt. "We just wanted a dog."

She could see the danger, but the poor boys could not. "I fully understand that you do. What fine lad does not want a pet to call his own? When I was your age, I desperately wanted a parrot I could teach to say, 'your wish is my command.' Except I did not have my front teeth when I read a book about parrots, so it always came out, 'your *with* is my command.' I am afraid I would have had the poorest speaking bird on the planet."

"I want a talkin' bird." The lad began flapping his arms as he turned in circles. The other boy did the same.

Standing, Elizabeth peered closer at them. Underneath a layer of dirt and mud were marks on their arms and legs in various shades of purple, yellow, brown, and green. She had no right to meddle in a situation that could lead to more harm to the children. Nevertheless, pure human kindness drove her to ask, "What are your names?"

"Jake." He pointed his finger behind him. "My brother is… uh, Johnny. He don't talk much, but he wants a dog too."

"Where is your uncle? You mentioned that Ralph is his name?" The only Ralph Elizabeth knew of who lived in the area was Ralph Simms, a recluse who fished part of the time, selling his catch by visiting the kitchens of the various landowners. Occasionally he rowed his skiff to the river Lea and beyond. Where he went or what he did was no concern to Elizabeth. It was well-known around the neighborhood that he drank when he was not in his boat.

The taller child shook his head, the fringe of his bangs hanging in his eyes. "Uncle Ralph musta got top-heavy late last night 'cause we woke to his castin' up…well, you must know what he was doin' this mornin'. We needed to get outta the cottage to let him sleep it off. He won't be fishin' t'day."

"Where are your parents? I should like to reunite you with them if I may."

His skinny shoulders drooped as he sighed. "Our mama isn't here anymore. She brought us on a ship from Potter County when she got sick and said we'd have to live with Uncle Ralph from now on." When he looked up at Elizabeth, tears pooled in his brown eyes, running down his dirty cheek. "I miss my mama. I want her to come back so we can get back on the ship and go home." He wiped his nose with his sleeve. "We had a dog there. His name was Max. He was a big black dog who only barked at strangers and bears. We had bears in Potter County. Big ones."

The other boy finally spoke. "I miss Mama too. And I miss my dog."

Elizabeth's fingers ached to rub the dirt off their cheeks. "I see. Where exactly is Potter County?"

"Pennsylvania."

Ah, this explained their accent. These two lads were far from anything familiar to them. Whoever was supposed to be caring for them was not tending to their duty.

"And your father?"

Neither boy would look at her. The taller one finally said, "His horse kicked him in the head. He didn't last long after. I hate horses!"

"Yeah, me too," the smaller one agreed.

"I am very sorry to hear about your parents." Digging

inside her purse, Elizabeth pulled out the last two orange candies, handing them to the brothers. "If you run your tongue over it slowly, it will last a long time."

"Aw, thanks. I'll try not to crunch down on it." After popping the sweetmeat into their mouths, they disappeared in the same direction as the dog.

Her heart broke a little. Pulling the string closed on her reticule, Elizabeth became aware of Mr. Darcy standing beside her.

"It is frightful to imagine being alone at their young age, is it not?"

She peered up at him only to discover he was still looking where the boys had headed. "I cannot imagine."

Mr. Darcy added, "I learned long ago that my responsibility was solely to those under my authority. The plight of the poor and suffering weighs on me to this day, especially those like these lads who have no one to act as their advocate."

Elizabeth felt the tendril of bitter anger growing inside of her. Why would a wealthy man like him not help the needy? Was he as cold-hearted as she had first thought him? She… no! In truth, she had no right to anger. She could say nothing since she had been taught from infancy that it was impossible for one individual or one family to save the world. Her father patiently explained to each of his daughters that bankrupting Longbourn to help the poor would put them in the same position. Rather than giving away all their funds to charity, they should be charitable, acting to help when needed in practical, beneficial ways. From then on, Elizabeth observed her mother sewing clothing for their tenants, people who worked hard to earn their keep. Cook took the garden and orchard's surplus to them. Her father would hire the men for extra work on the estate.

Rethinking his comment about Jake and Johnny, she realized that just as the lads' circumstances pained her, they also pained him.

"Miss Elizabeth, I shall ask Bingley's steward if he knows who is keeping the children. Perhaps something could be done for their care."

Her breath caught in her throat. "You will?"

"Indeed."

At the assembly, the few words he uttered were acerbic. Yet, on this day, he was kindness itself. *Who was this man?*

CHAPTER 6

Elizabeth's return to Mr. Dale's bookshop was both eye-opening and confusing.

"I am terribly sorry, Miss Lizzy, but there will be no more charges until the Bennet account is settled." Mr. Dale took the new publication by *A Lady* and placed it under the counter.

"There must be some confusion. Are you certain?"

"I am." He was adamant.

Elizabeth was grateful there were no witnesses to the conversation. Jane joined their other sisters to visit the bakery. Mr. Bingley and Mr. Darcy followed.

It was with cold trepidation that she walked the one-mile distance to Longbourn. Little clues that she had previously ignored fell into place. At the sweet shop, the proprietor asked if she would be paying for her purchase. Fortunately, she had coins in her reticule, assuming the owner was in need. She had ignored Lydia and Kitty begging her to ask their father for their allowance for the past several weeks; Elizabeth suddenly realized that it had been before the last quarter since she received her pin money. Her mother made excuses for not serving a dessert with each meal by claiming she did not want to see extra roundness on her daughters until they all found husbands.

What was happening? Whatever it was had to be a dreadful mistake. She fully expected her father to be upset at the affront. "What sort of game do you have with Mr. Dale that he refuses me the latest release of my favorite author?"

Her father's chin dropped to his chest. His eyes closed. Setting aside the book he had been reading, Thomas Bennet said, "Longbourn's household accounts have been stretched to the limits, I am afraid."

"How? Why?" Elizabeth did not understand. There had been no grand purchases. They had not gone on holiday. The harvest had come and gone. The crops were sold. The income put…where? In the Bank of England, which long held Longbourn's accounts? "Can you not withdraw funds from the bank?"

"What funds?" her father scoffed. "If our tenants do not pay their rents on time, Longbourn may be lost to us long before I depart this earth."

"What?" Stunned, Elizabeth's hand went to her chest. "Are you saying that we need to retrench? Where has our income gone? I do not understand."

He shrugged. "This is not your concern, Lizzy. Bennets have been at Longbourn for the past two hundred years. I cannot see us being evicted or tossed into debtors' prison within the next several months."

"Papa! Please tell me this is a joke." Elizabeth refused to blink should she miss the twinkle in his eye. When none appeared, she pressed her hands to her churning stomach. "To whom are we indebted? The house and land are entailed, so you cannot have borrowed against them, can you? Would you?"

His sigh shook his shoulders. "Do not say a word to your

sisters, Elizabeth." He removed his spectacles and swiped his hand over his face. "Years ago, I gambled and lost against a powerful man who has long wanted everything I possess. You are correct that I have no right to sell the property.

"Nevertheless, some unscrupulous lenders will extend a loan against the estate for my lifetime. Any income generated by Longbourn is paid with interest accrued almost by the minute. Once I die, they have no claim against the property, so it goes to my heir unencumbered."

"What of the debt? Who would be required to pay these unscrupulous men? Would we, your wife and daughters, become slaves to them to be used at their discretion? Papa, who do you owe and where did the money go?"

He slumped over his desk. "According to the terms of purchase, I cannot say."

She gasped.

"Lizzy, I was confident in the transaction since the man with whom I negotiated was known to me. Gossip of his downfall and his selling what I assumed were his family's priceless treasures led me to believe he could be trusted. He was desperate. I knew that if I could hold onto the map for enough years, the increase to its value would see my wife and daughters set for their lifetimes."

"What happened?" Elizabeth asked, though she was loathe to hear his response.

"About ten years ago or so, a wealthy gentleman approached me with a generous offer for the map. Upon close examination, he recognized one of the names in the legend as being too recent for a map of that age. The only thing he left Longbourn with was his disappointment. I was left with my dreams crushed."

"Who was this man?"

"I do not recall. It has been so long ago."

"Papa, cannot you bring a claim against the seller?"

"I would bring trouble upon us if I sought justice."

"There has to be something we can do."

"Lizzy, what is done is done. I will thank you to remember that you have no say in any decision I have made. Your mother has been told the same. These matters have a way of working out. You shall see."

Despite being the first time in her memory that her father had spoken to her harshly, she could not restrain her tongue. "How, Papa? How will you keep us from Marshalsea? Have you a plan?"

Dropping his forehead to his palms, he muttered, "Not yet. However, I am not without intelligence. Something will occur to me, I am sure."

She wanted to vomit. How could this have happened? *Good heavens!* What could she possibly do to help her family?"

* * *

TWO DAYS of heavy rain kept the Netherfield party at home. On the third day, they dared to venture away from the estate. Sir William Lucas hosted a gathering that was to include the Bennet family. Darcy had yet to meet Mr. Bennet and was curious about the man who raised a daughter like Miss Elizabeth.

He mentally chastised himself. Miss Elizabeth Bennet was far enough below his sphere that he should have dismissed her immediately from his mind. She meant nothing to him and would never mean anything other than a temporary diversion while he was with the Bingleys.

The Lucases had five children at home, Charlotte, Robert, John, Albert, and Maria. In his mind, Darcy attempted to match Sir William's sons with the lads on the *HMS Voyager*. However, that day he had paid more attention to the captain of the adventure, the condition of her raft, and her being in the river than the mutinous lads.

"Welcome to Lucas Lodge." Sir William was a portly man with a jovial smile. "We are awaiting the arrival of the Bennets. Please join us for refreshments."

Immediately one of the sons approached Darcy, intent on impressing him. Robert Lucas was a bore.

"At university, I was the top of my class. The other students looked to me for help when they floundered on their examinations. Agriculture and agronomy were my specialties since I will one day inherit Lucas Lodge." He clasped his lapels as he rocked back and forth on his heels. "Say, Darcy, I suppose you are letting your land lie fallow for the winter like we decided to do. Other landowners in the area chose to throw away their funds on purchasing beets, turnips, and cabbages to put into their soil. What a waste…"

He droned on and on and on.

Having not given the younger man permission to address him informally, Darcy ignored Robert Lucas's prattle, moving away from him with no regrets. He wanted to shake his head. *Not plant winter crops? Imbecile!* Why would a landowner not plant vegetables that would overwinter? If the soil were healthy, a good amount of mulch from the straw removed from the coops and stables would protect the growing plants, providing food for the house and the animals in early spring. Robert Lucas might have been at the top of his class, but he was an idiot.

Standing at the fireplace, Darcy observed the other two sons of Sir William attempting to attract Miss Bingley's interest. When her mouth was closed, she was quite lovely. Additionally, she had twenty thousand as her dowry. However, her shrewish nature was revealed the instant she spoke, rendering her unattractive and not worth all her wealth, including compounded interest. She pretended to ignore the two brothers, glancing at Darcy to see if he resented the attentions of the younger men. *As if he would!*

The youngest Lucas daughter sat quietly beside her mother while the eldest watched the door for the rest of their guests, as was he.

Before he could consider his motives, the Bennets swept into the room. Robert Lucas rushed to Miss Bennet's side, just ahead of Bingley. They were like two bucks after the same doe, so intent on their purpose that they failed to realize how much they frightened the lady. And into the fray stepped Miss Elizabeth.

Standing between the two men, separating them like Moses did the Red Sea, she said, "Gentlemen, might I beg one of you to provide Jane with a cup of tea? The chill of the air cannot be healthy for one so fair."

"Lizzy!" her sister whispered. "I am well."

"Yes, you are." Miss Elizabeth grinned, her eyes twinkling in the candlelight as Bingley and Lucas hurried away. "However, now we can greet our hosts and the rest of the guests without fear of you being trampled. Come, Mama is already with Lady Lucas and Charlotte."

Taking her sister's arm, she led Miss Bennet away from the tea table where Bingley and Lucas jostled the pot, trying to wait upon the lady.

Miss Lucas welcomed the two eldest Bennets with open friendliness rather than a polite salutation. The younger Bennet girls swarmed around Miss Maria. Their laughter made it difficult for him to hear the exchange between the elderly females.

Good lord! Was he eavesdropping? How below him! With purpose, Darcy distanced himself by moving to the other side of the massive stones surrounding the fire.

He was never comfortable in society unknown to him. With his position of elevated rank, he was not required to give anyone the time of day. His father never did. Nonetheless, Darcy's very association with Bingley, whose ancestors had made their fortune in trade, showed how some of his prideful prejudices dissolved since inheriting the Darcy mantle.

Being content to stand away from the others and observe, he was perturbed when Sir William approached.

"Mr. Darcy, I suppose you are often at St. James. Why, since I was blessed with my knighthood, I have been at least once each year. I am quite surprised that we have not encountered each other before now."

Since there were very few things Darcy loathed more than the poppycock's parading around the Prince Regent, Darcy stared coldly at the man. "I never attend St. James." He looked away from his host, not desiring to witness his disappointment. Changing the subject, he asked, "Is Mr. Bennet not expected?"

Sir William shook his head, the color returning to his face. "Bennet rarely leaves his book room. There have been rumors—"

"Of which I have no interest," Darcy stated plainly, which ended the conversation.

Glancing at Miss Elizabeth, he saw she had drawn especially close to Miss Lucas, her expression solemn as she spoke with her friend. Miss Lucas was likewise fully engaged in the conversation. They failed to notice the two men trying to press a brimming, hot cup of tea on the lady seated next to them. Miss Elizabeth ignored Darcy, which was not unexpected.

What were they discussing? Before he could give the matter too much attention, Miss Bingley approached.

"I can guess what you are thinking," she said as she stepped closer to him.

With the wall behind him and the heavy stones next to

him, he was unable to escape her—a foolish miscalculation on his part.

"I cannot imagine why you believe I would allow you to be privy to my thoughts, Miss Bingley. Pardon me." He walked to where Bingley attempted to engage Miss Bennet in conversation.

Would the supper hour never arrive? He forced his jaw to relax to keep from loudly gritting his teeth.

"Mr. Darcy," Miss Elizabeth addressed him, bringing him a spot of relief too short-lived. "Charlotte and I were discussing—"

Three out of the four younger girls chose that moment to interrupt. "This evening is frightfully dull. Lizzy, play so we can dance."

"No, Lydia." Miss Elizabeth stood and faced the younger girl. In a quieter tone, she added, "We shall patiently wait until our hosts suggest the entertainment. Let us remember that this is someone else's house. We are the guests."

The girls huffed before returning to the sofa, where they huddled again.

The urge to flee obliged Darcy to calculate how long it would take to request the carriage and return to Netherfield Park…alone. Pain throbbed at the base of his skull. He required a quiet room, semi-darkness, and a snifter of fine brandy.

"Mr. Darcy, if you have a moment," Miss Elizabeth said.

He sighed heavily, rubbing at his temples. "I am afraid I should not have come. I beg your pardon, but in all honesty, the neighborhood gossip does not interest me since I am unacquainted with any of the parties. I am sure you understand."

Her lips pressed together until they were a thin line, and the knuckles of her clasped hands were white. "I see. Charlotte had helpful information about the little boys we met outside the bookshop. Since you lack interest, I shall know how to act. Good evening, sir." She curtsied.

Before she turned away from him, her eyes caught his. The flame shooting from her glance threatened to singe the fibers of his garments. He was surprised that he did not smell smoke.

He wanted to talk about the lads, but it was too late. Again, he had been too abrupt, his assumptions poorly stated. *Blast!* If only his head did not feel like a blacksmith wielded his hammer on the back of his skull. Calling for the carriage, he excused himself and left.

The coach had not yet passed through Meryton before Darcy wondered, did Miss Elizabeth believe his departure was for his benefit or hers?

* * *

Of all the rude, arrogant males she had ever met, Mr. Darcy was the worst. Despite the occasional glimpses of empathy and pleasantness, her final impression of him was poor. What happened to sour him? Or was he born that way? She shook her head since the man was none of her concern.

Charlotte Lucas had a quick wit with a hint of sarcasm. "It is rather entertaining to watch my brothers try to tempt and woo Jane and Miss Bingley. I fear their success is limited by their complete lack of finesse."

"Do you think so?" Elizabeth teased. "Why, the salient question is whether the two of us have any clue how to attract a male."

Charlotte laughed, as did Elizabeth.

"Mr. Darcy's eyes rarely left you during the short time he was here. To soothe any concerns on your part, I checked your face for blemishes and your gown for stains. None were visible, in case you wondered."

Elizabeth snickered. "I believe we have finally met a man truly unable to be pleased. The plain fact is that if he was looking at me, he was entirely obtuse to the true beauty in the room. Not once did he indicate that he was willing to push Robbie or Mr. Bingley aside. Nor did he pay any attention to Miss Bingley's efforts to capture his attention. Perhaps he is so happy with his own company that he cannot stand anyone else's."

"Oh, Lizzy, I hear a hint of bitterness in your tone. Is it Mr. Darcy that has caused this, or something else?"

Elizabeth turned quickly to look directly at her friend. "What have you heard, Charlotte?"

"I have heard rumors. I imagine it will not be long, and everyone will know."

Elizabeth gazed into the kind eyes of her closest friend. To lose Longbourn was devastating. To have her family torn apart by debt collectors was unimaginable. "What can we do, Charlotte?"

"I do not know." Her eyes darted to where Mr. Bingley stood next to Jane. "While you can, encouraging Jane to express affection to move Mr. Bingley to act quickly would not be amiss."

Elizabeth was horrified. "She would never—"

"She may have no choice. None of you may."

Elizabeth's active imagination could easily conjure their future. Neither of her parents appeared willing to sacrifice since they decided to keep up appearances. Yet now was not the time to hide from the shame. It was time to act. Charlotte was correct. Better a kind man like their new neighbor than a grasping oaf who would use every advantage against her sisters. Jane would need to marry. Kitty and Lydia needed to know what was happening so their insistence on filling their closets and ribbon boxes would stop. Mary would need to extend herself to others rather than constantly seeking self-improvement.

What of herself? Elizabeth might need to go into service, which meant she would never marry. She would be separated from her family to live wherever she was offered employment.

Elizabeth's turbulent emotions stirred. *What was she to do?*

CHAPTER 7

Several endless days later, Darcy rode the along the fence separating Netherfield Park from Longbourn along with Bingley and his steward, Mr. Morris.

Although Bingley was the lessee, it was Darcy who Mr. Morris consulted about the potential for flooding. A massive pile of downed trees snarled together into a tangle of limbs close to the mouth of a small trickle leading to where he first spotted Miss Elizabeth fourteen years prior. Behind the naturally formed dam was a pond threatening to overflow into the fields with the next heavy rains. Although the pond was on Longbourn's land, the water, should the dam break, would cover Netherfield's property and beyond.

"Have you spoken with the steward at Longbourn?" Darcy asked.

"There is no steward, sir." Mr. Morris removed a handkerchief to wipe his brow. "There has not been a land manager at Longbourn since Mr. Bennet took possession about a quarter century ago. Fortunately for Mr. Bennet, one of his tenants had an eye for which crops to plant and enough insight into Hertfordshire weather patterns to know when to seed and when to harvest. Old Angus Swearingen died last spring. With him gone and our cool summer, the harvest this year at Longbourn was even poorer than ours."

"I am sorry to hear it," Darcy admitted, although anger rather than sadness churned inside him. Time and again, he watched estates fall into trouble when the person in charge failed to plan for the future. Due diligence was typically the only thing separating prosperity and poverty. "Are the Bennets in trouble?"

Mr. Morris looked to Bingley, gathering the last of the season's flowers for Miss Bennet. "Rumors are rife in the community. Five girls to marry off, and all Mr. Bennet does is buy more books."

Darcy shook his head. This did not bode well for Miss Bennet's and Miss Elizabeth's prospects. However, neither lady was his concern.

He said, "Then let us hope we can stir him from his bookroom long enough to have him take control of the tangled mess in front of us, or both properties will suffer."

The steward shook his head. "I wish you success, sir."

* * *

ELIZABETH MEANDERED through the downstairs rooms examining every painting, piece of furniture, rug, and needlework project on the floor, walls, shelves, and tables. All in all, the Bennets had nothing new or of intrinsic value to sell. Her mother had one or two insignificant pieces of jewelry that would bring little if forced to part with them. They had no extra servants to let go to save additional funds. Where had the money gone?

Just as the assembly had openly discussed the incomes of Mr. Darcy and Mr. Bingley, anyone who wanted to know would easily guess that Longbourn's annual income was approximately two thousand. Although she was not privy to the accounts, each daughter received an increase in their pin money as soon as she came out in society. They had all come to depend on the stability of their household. To discover it was a sham was terrifying.

Despite this, hope rose inside her each time she entered a room. Each time she departed, she felt a blow to her chest.

How unfair that this had been kept a secret from them. Although, in truth, what would it have changed for any of them to know that disaster loomed? At least she would not have allowed Lydia to "borrow" the coins she saved from the last time her father paid out pin money.

Her father had not disclosed where the money he borrowed had gone nor for what purpose. Did he keep secrets for the shame of single-handedly putting them on the brink of ruin? Was it something illegal or immoral? Elizabeth could not imagine the possibility since he was more a creature of habit than anyone she knew.

Additionally, he rarely left home. The few times he did was to purchase another box of books and old maps. He was the least nefarious male she knew. Except, he admitted that he gambled and lost. Was it cards? He never played. A chess match? She gasped. He competed regularly via the post, sending his next move by letter to his competitor. Did they play for money? Elizabeth would never have suspected him of being a gambler, but she must admit she did not know her father as she thought. No, he said it was a transaction. *A map?* Had he purchased a stolen or counterfeit item? Surely not!

She wanted to scoff at her foolishness, for she had long feared it would be her youngest sister, Lydia, whose reckless and bold attitude would bring them down. Never would she have imagined her father would fail them.

She sighed, wiping a tear from the corner of her eye on her sleeve. He was the parent she favored far more than her mother. He welcomed her to his book room, taught her to read and write, helped her appreciate the beauty of the printed word, and treated her to lengthy debates where she formed strong opinions and attitudes. For her lifetime, he had been her constant where she could run when troubled.

What had happened? How had matters come to this?

With no answers available to her, for the first time, Elizabeth knew helplessness. Nevertheless, she was not without hope. Her father was intelligent, as was she. *Something must be done.* After consulting her uncles, one a local attorney and the other in the import/export business, a path of recovery might come to light and bail them out, keeping the family out of the hedgerows or debtor's prison. She would speak to her father immediately.

* * *

Bingley grinned all the way to Longbourn. He could barely control his horse with one hand holding six brightly colored chrysanthemums he had discovered close to a fence post. The stems were bound with his folded handkerchief and retied enough times to attempt a stylish bow. From Darcy's perspective, the bouquet was a paltry offering. Yet the lady, if she was kind, might overlook any flaws. Bingley was entirely blind to the flowers not being perfect.

Darcy remained silent until they arrived at the neighboring estate.

Longbourn's main house was well-kept and tidy. The shrubs leading up to the front door were trimmed and neat, and the stone walkway recently swept. Once inside, Darcy could not help but note the heavy furniture that had been popular a decade past. Paintings and framed drawings looked to be by amateurs, the Bennet girls, perhaps. The carpets, although spotless, were well-worn. All in all, it looked like a comfortable home.

When invited into the master's study, Darcy barely kept his mouth from dropping open. There was not a single inch where books were not stacked or lined up in rows. Rarely had he seen the like, no matter how devoted the bibliophile. Discretely checking some titles, he saw old and new volumes on various subjects. His libraries at Pemberley and Darcy House were the work of generations. He took personal delight in a regular review of their contents, so he knew value when he saw it. Mr. Bennet's library was a treasure trove.

Instead of thrilling him to see so many valuable tomes in one place, it stirred his ire. If the rumors were true, Mr. Bennet of Longbourn had selfishly catered to his desires at the cost of his family and estate. *Shame on him!*

Mr. Bennet came from around his desk, extending his hand to Bingley and then Darcy. Nodding at the steward, he said, "Gentlemen, welcome to Longbourn."

Darcy guessed that the man's age was close to his father's, had he lived. He was tall and slender, but his handshake was soft. Darcy wanted to wipe his palm on the side of his trousers.

"How might I be of assistance?" The master of Longbourn looked at the flowers in Bingley's hand. He quipped, "Are those for me?"

Bingley blushed, then began, "These are for Miss Bennet." He placed them on a stack of books. "Say, there are large timbers and limbs near the fence line between our properties threatening collapse. A rather massive pond developed behind the dam. I was…we were wondering if we might assist you in disassembling it to keep the water from flooding into Netherfield."

Darcy was proud of his friend for taking the lead.

"I see." Mr. Bennet removed his glasses and wiped the lenses on a cloth. "Have you considered what would happen if it were suddenly demolished? Why that would do more harm, I believe. Therefore, nature will take its course."

Darcy sat back, trying and failing to distance himself from that opinion.

Bingley again attempted to offer reason. "Sir, if we pull down small portions at a time, the natural path of the water would lead directly to the river mitigating the damage."

"Ah, but there is the problem. You see, I am not skilled in physics or engineering. Unless someone knows what is behind those logs, which are all underwater, how do we know which to pull first? I rather think it is like Spillikins. I have never been good at the game. My Lizzy now, she routinely beats her sisters when they play. Possibly, she would be the one to ask. Should I call her?"

The three men from Netherfield sat in silence.

Darcy was livid. The master of Longbourn would rather ask a girl, his daughter, to be responsible. It was untenable! "Mr. Bennet, controlling the water flow is the key. If we pulled from the top, it lessens the chance of the bottom giving way."

Mr. Bennet waved his hand. "No. I shall not have anyone tearing apart Longbourn's land. The dam is naturally occurring. It sits below a spring that has been there for centuries. The runoff from the almost constant rain has increased the water level. None of this was caused by me. Therefore, it shall be left undisturbed. I want nothing to do with altering that which has already happened."

"But this is nonsensical! What do you imagine could be behind the logs? Bingley's plan is sound to manage the improvement in stages," Darcy blurted. "An influx of water would flood the fields, Mr. Bennet. Think what a sudden wall of water would do to those who live near the river. It could be the death of many."

Mr. Bennet shook his head. "Then we shall hope the winter rains and snow are not heavy. As it is, those downstream should not have built their homes close to the river's edge. I cannot feel a responsibility to anyone outside my own people." Mr. Bennet stood. "If that is all, gentlemen?"

They had been dismissed.

Of all the stupid...! It was no wonder Darcy was jaded in his outlook. There were far too many landlords like Mr. Bennet, and far too many others hurt because of it. Wishing he had never come to Hertfordshire, Darcy left the main house hoping never to return. Perhaps it was best to encourage Bingley to depart Netherfield Park. The lease was for one year. The toll for paying for a property he could not use for twelve months was monumental. However, being out from under the responsibility of the impending disaster was priceless.

CHAPTER 8

Elizabeth fretted day and night about their situation. A full week had gone by since she exchanged words with her father. The shame of their finances kept her from Meryton. In spite of her warning, one by one, her younger sisters tried to purchase baubles and lace on credit as they had always done. One by one, they had returned embarrassed and confused. Yet, her father staunchly refused to offer any explanation.

Neighbors no longer called. Even their aunt and uncle Phillips, who happened to be Meryton's sole attorney, did not make the one-mile journey to see their closest family members.

Francine Bennet was distraught. Her groaning set everyone on edge except for her husband, who remained closeted behind his study doors.

Mrs. Hill, Longbourn's faithful housekeeper, whispered to the mistress that Mr. Bingley and Mr. Darcy had presented themselves to the master, leaving Longbourn before either man could offer for one of her daughters. This added insult to injury in the mind of Mrs. Bennet.

Elizabeth wondered about the purpose of their visit. From their housekeeper's reports, neither man looked pleased when they left. What business did they have with her father? Elizabeth could not begin to imagine what brought them to Longbourn. She was curious, but not enough to approach her father. Lately, he was in a foul mood.

She hesitated. Were they there to press a claim for money? Had her father borrowed from someone associated with Netherfield Park? The thought was mortifying. She needed answers but knew aught how to obtain them.

Although it was Elizabeth's nature to find joy in almost any situation, little brought her delight. November arrived with freezing winds and almost constant downpours. Even the weather seemed to plot against her, further dampening her typically sunny disposition.

One bright spot was an invitation Jane received from Miss Bingley inviting her to tea with the ladies at Netherfield Park. All five sisters joined in rifling through Jane's gowns and *accoutrement* to choose her attire. For once, there was no bickering. Not even Lydia insisted it was her opinion that mattered most. Her alteration in character was a reminder that Elizabeth was not the only one affected by their changed circumstances.

Francine Bennet stood by the window, rubbing her palms together. "Mark my words. It shall rain by the time Jane arrives. If she takes the horse instead of the carriage, Miss Bingley must invite her to stay at Netherfield Park. Thus, she will see Mr. Bingley after all."

"Mama!" all five girls balked.

Elizabeth pleaded, "It would not do to have Jane's beauty diminished by arriving soaked to her skin. What would Mr. Bingley think?"

"Pshaw! He will want to hurry home from his other plans to care for his guest. I know these things, Lizzy, where you do not." Turning to check that all was well with Jane's appearance, she added, "I shall come to see you early tomorrow to make sure that Mr. Bingley is aware of his responsibility to tend to your care. Although after his efforts to find those pitiful flowers, I believe he is as close as he could be to making an offer."

From experience, Elizabeth knew it was fruitless to argue with a parent who saw matters from one point of view—hers.

As their mother predicted, the rain began in earnest within five minutes of Jane's departure. Later that evening, a note was received that Jane was indeed ill. Instead of her mother's presence, Jane wanted Elizabeth.

* * *

ELIZABETH'S ARRIVAL WAS ILL-TIMED, and she could not help but overhear the conversation around Netherfield's breakfast table. Her efforts to distract herself in the few seconds until she was announced failed spectacularly.

"I cannot imagine any lady of refinement riding a plow horse," said Caroline Bingley. "It shows a country sort of manners if I do say so myself. What do you think, Mr. Darcy? Would you allow Georgiana to ride to a neighboring property in a heavy rain with no maid to accompany her?"

"I would not."

Bingley interjected, "I see matters quite differently, Caroline. To me, her using whatever transport was available showed a desire to accept your invitation and spend time in your company. It speaks well of Miss Bennet's good manners."

Elizabeth was delighted to discover that her initial impression of their neighbor was wrong. Although he did not speak up to defend her at the assembly, his doing so for Jane bespoke the courage of a gentleman.

The butler announced, "Miss Elizabeth Bennet to see Miss Jane Bennet, sir."

Mr. Bingley and Mr. Darcy stood. The others at the table looked at her like she was a banshee arrived to cast doom and gloom over the household.

"Miss Elizabeth, I am certain your sister will be happy you are here." Mr. Bingley waved toward the table. "Before you go upstairs, mightn't we share our repast?"

Elizabeth curtseyed. "I thank you, but no. I need to see Jane if you please."

As she waited for Mr. Bingley's reply, her eyes scanned the others. Mr. and Mrs. Hursts' attention was on their plates. Miss Bingley's lips pressed into a straight line, her eyes pinched at the corners. Mr. Darcy was…smiling? *Whatever was he about?* Ridiculous man!

* * *

FITZWILLIAM DARCY WAS PLEASED with her arrival sans family.

Miss Bingley, on the other hand, was livid. As soon as Miss Elizabeth departed the room, she pointed out the obvious; the lady walked from Longbourn to Netherfield Park, a distance of three miles. Yes, her hems were dirty, and her walking boots needed a good cleaning. In Darcy's opinion, her eyes were brightened by the exercise.

He was determined to speak to her, to apologize again for insulting her and for his failure to listen to her at Lucas Lodge. Before she returned to Longbourn, Darcy would instruct his grooms to be ready to carry her and possibly her sister in his town coach. He doubted she had ever traveled in such luxury.

With a purpose in mind, Darcy returned to his chambers. His skill in formulating appropriate wording on paper was far better than speaking extemporaneously. Thus, he spent the next few hours writing different approaches to his apology. He wanted there to be no misunderstanding. Without a doubt, she saw him as less than a gentleman, which was not the truth of the matter. He wanted, no, he needed her to see him as he truly was. Why this mattered so much to him, he dared not consider. For now, a well-delivered apology would suffice.

* * *

"Oh, my dear Jane. You are ever so obedient. You became ill exactly as Mama planned. She is thrilled."

Jane sneezed. Even with pale skin and a red-tipped nose, she was the picture of loveliness.

"Lizzy, they are taking good care of me. Mrs. Hurst and Miss Bingley have already waited upon me this morning. They spoke of the many people of their acquaintance from the first circles. Of course, I know none of them, but it was a kindness that they shared information with me that is very important to them."

Elizabeth shook her head, "Only you would see their attentions as kindness. Be that as it may, I will confess that your pink nose matches the roses in your cheeks, and the water in your eyes renders them a brilliant blue. Mr. Bingley is sure to be impressed with the deep register of your tone. Why, you will need to sing the baritone parts at services on Sunday, I think."

Jane's flushed face and teary eyes were evidence of her misery. Her voice was scratchy from a raw throat. "The maid Miss Bingley assigned me has passed several messages to me from Mr. Bingley asking about my health, offering to send for his physician in London if I felt it would benefit me. Oh, Lizzy! He is everything a gentleman should be. I was mortified to arrive yesterday. Our old plow horse ignored the thunder and lightning. Nothing I did moved him any faster than his slow, steady gait. I was three-quarters of an hour in the rain. It was unfortunate that Mr. Bingley, Mr. Darcy, and Mr. Hurst took into account the bad weather and stayed home. Thus, they were here when I arrived, sodden and miserable."

"I am sorry," Elizabeth commiserated. "Mama declared that you will be engaged by the time you return to Longbourn. I fear she is resting our family's salvation on your shoulders."

Jane swiped the moisture from her eyes. "Is it really that bad?"

Elizabeth's nature was to face trials head-on. "Yes, Jane. Even Papa is hoping Mr. Bingley will come up to scratch."

"I cannot make him love me." Jane pushed herself up until she leaned on the headboard. "You know me, Lizzy. I cannot nor will not put myself forward, just as you would not. Would I prefer to wed someone who appears to be as kind as Mr. Bingley? Yes, but only once he has proven himself to be genuine. I would expect him to wait to determine the same about me."

Elizabeth sat next to her, brushing the wispy hair from her sister's brow. She whispered, "I would rather go into service or marry a stranger than see you unequally matched. He defended you to his sisters."

"He did?"

"You are pleased, I can tell." Elizabeth poured cool water to ease Jane's throat. "Pray, allow me to repeat the portion of the conversation I overheard. Before I do, I will confess that Mr. Bingley's comments revealed much good about him. You have loved a much stupider man. Do you recall Simon Peterson? Your bag was packed for a quick elopement to Gretna Green. Had I not stopped you, who knows where you would be now."

Jane snickered. "I was only ten."

"And I was eight. But I knew that boy would never be able to support a wife. He spent more time throwing rocks into the river than poring over his schoolbooks."

"I thought he was so grown-up. He was almost twelve, after all."

Elizabeth laughed. Sobering, she said, "Jane, let us make a pact between us that, whatever is to come of us, we will do all within our power to make decisions that will improve our chances for happiness."

"I agree."

* * *

Later that evening, Darcy's hand dipped into his coat pocket to ensure his notes were still there. He was soon to be called to the evening meal, which would be his last opportunity that day to arrange a private moment with Miss Elizabeth to explain to her his actions and comments. He did not want the day to end without the hope of peace between them.

Unfortunately, her sister's health took a turn for the worse. Miss Elizabeth took a tray in Miss Bennet's chambers.

The following day, Mrs. Bennet and the rest of her daughters arrived. Miss Elizabeth spent the whole of their visit attempting to corral her mother and Miss Lydia's boisterousness. In the ensuing uproar, there was no opportunity for conversation.

However, by the evening, a slight improvement in Miss Bennet's cough allowed her sister to join the group in the drawing room.

"Miss Eliza," Caroline Bingley simpered. "I would have thought a hearty country girl could have shrugged off pouring rain and splattered mud with no ill effects. My friends in Town would never present themselves as guests as rumpled as we have seen here in Hertfordshire. Is this the standard for female conduct?"

Darcy's glance darted to Bingley, hoping his friend would stop his sister from showing her claws.

"Say, Caroline," Bingley responded. "Is it not true that you and Louisa used to run and jump in the mud when we lived in Manchester?" To Miss Elizabeth, he said, "Our grandfather and father owned fabric mills. We lived not far from the factories where we often joined the other children for play."

"You are speaking of many, many years ago, Charles. As an adult woman, I would never countenance having a shoddy appearance."

"Caroline! That was unkind," Bingley reprimanded to no effect.

Miss Bingley brushed her hands together, a sure sign that she would ignore the rebuke. "Mr. Darcy, how is your sister? The little tables she painted at Pemberley are magnificent. She is a proficient on the pianoforte. Why, few ladies in Town can compare to dear Georgiana's skill."

Darcy was angry. Miss Bingley was pretending a familiarity she did not possess. "My sister, Miss Darcy, has many natural talents. Nonetheless, she would be uncomfortable with any comparisons made to others, especially to individuals unknown to her."

"I beg your pardon, sir." Miss Bingley purred. "My goal was to compliment. If I did not make myself clear, I apologize."

Darcy noticed Miss Elizabeth's interest in the book he left on the small table next to her at the end of the sofa.

"Are you familiar with the works of *A Lady,* Miss Elizabeth? My sister was so excited to read *Sense and Sensibility* that I needed to purchase the three volumes myself."

She looked up from the book she was holding. "I beg your pardon, sir. I did not know this was your personal copy." Setting it back on the table, Miss Elizabeth prepared to stand.

He hurried to stop her. "No, please enjoy the book. I brought it down for others to read. The other two volumes are also available. I completed them last evening."

Her fingers danced over the book's spine. "Having many sisters of my own, I am eager to see if Elinor and Marianne are much like Jane and myself." Her eyes twinkled. "What do you think, Mr. Darcy? From the little you know of us, is there much resemblance?"

"Who is this *A Lady?*" Caroline Bingley insisted. "Surely, if Georgiana Darcy is interested, the characters would be patterned after debutantes with elevated rank, not country females who prance about the neighborhood unchaperoned."

"Caroline!" Bingley hissed.

Darcy saw the exact moment when Miss Elizabeth registered the insult, for her shoulders pressed back, her chin lifted ever so slightly, and her eyes fastened on Miss Bingley.

Miss Elizabeth said, "I do not know that anyone other than her immediate circle and the publisher knows the correct identity of the author, Miss Bingley. Whether she is from London or one of the shires is unknown. What I do comprehend from the opinion of my aunt, who obtained a copy the day it was available, the talent of the individual who wrote the story is exceptional. Since Mr. Darcy has admitted to finishing the book, perhaps he can reassure us as to its suitability for our eyes. What think you, sir?"

He admitted, "I think far too much is made of the importance of living in Town. The majority of the tale takes place in a country setting. The relationship between the sisters is complex. What is most concerning to them is their struggle to provide for themselves when circumstances outside their control rob them of their security. Although they are no less genteel, they become reliant upon others, which decidedly lowers their prospects. Yet, they each find happiness in their own way."

Miss Elizabeth's reaction captured his attention. The color rushed from her cheeks, and the knuckles and tips of her fingers whitened where she gripped the book.

Laying the tome carefully aside, she stood. "I beg your pardon. I have been too long away from Jane."

Moments later, she was gone.

What happened? Reconsidering each word, Darcy worried that he had given too much of the story away, that her reading enjoyment disappeared under….no, he had not told her precisely how *Sense and Sensibility* would end. He mentioned reduced circumstances and….*Blast!* Ugly suspicions crept into his thinking. Were the Bennets in trouble? Had one of her sisters crossed the line of propriety where the whole family teetered on the brink of ruin? Had their father squandered….?

Pieces of a puzzle began to align. Mr. Bennet's piles of expensive books would drain a small estate. Netherfield's steward mentioned that Longbourn's harvest had been poor. Mr. Bennet had also said he collected old maps. His father collected old maps as well.

Thinking back, Darcy finally knew why his father must have stopped in Meryton. Mr. Bennet had something Gerald Darcy wanted. His father's disgust and anger when they departed the small village surely meant that the asking price was ridiculously high or the map was not original.

The cost of a well-copied fake was expensive. His uncle's lifestyle had been supported by selling…. *Oh, good lord!* He hoped Mr. Bennet had not done business with Lord

Matlock! If so, the interest payments alone would quickly empty the coffers of Longbourn.

If he had, it was no wonder the parents encouraged Miss Bennet to ride in the rain. Were they hoping to entrap Bingley, a man who would never suspect a nefarious strategy from a neighbor?

Darcy ran his hands over his face. Was Miss Bennet complicit? Her embarrassment upon her arrival appeared genuine. What of Miss Elizabeth? Was her attendance to care for her sister a pretense? Was it her goal to promote a match? Or was she trying to attract a bigger fish? Him?

His stomach churned. His apology was forgotten in his pocket. Any interest in making peace with the second Bennet daughter was gone.

CHAPTER 9

Jane had a restless night, which meant that Elizabeth did as well. Gathering her outer garments from a footman, she hurried from Netherfield Park to the one place she always found peace—the river.

Somewhere above them, a leaf dropped into the swirling water, rising to the crest, and dropping over the rocks below. Elizabeth felt like that burnished leaf, tossed and turned with no destination. She preferred to have both feet on the ground.

The first volume of *Sense and Sensibility* was the book she tried to purchase at Mr. Dale's bookshop. Now that she knew her situation was strikingly similar to what the Dashwood ladies faced, she no longer desired to read their tale. Unless there were clues the author revealed that could help her family personally, she would never touch the book again. The Bennets' lives had turned into a gothic novel, which often left the heroine writhing in agony at the end.

Would that happen to them? To her?

A servant interrupted her thoughts. "Miss, your sister is awake and asking for you."

"Thank you." When she returned to the house, she spied a figure in the shadows of one of the upstairs windows. The man was tall and slender. Mr. Darcy. He would be the last person she wanted to learn of their troubles.

* * *

THE RUSTLING of the paper in his pocket caught Darcy's attention. The carefully penned apology reminded him that he had misjudged Miss Elizabeth Bennet. Was he doing so again? Perhaps, his conclusions were in error. Was her concern for her sister's health the only thing on her mind?

Good grief! Was he so insensitive that he looked for harm when there was none?

Pulling the parchment from his pocket, he reread his words.

Miss Elizabeth, I was in error when I publicly claimed you to be intolerable. As a gentleman, my behavior toward a lady should always be in her best interests. Therefore, I beg your forgiveness while promising you that I will strive to do better in the future.

He was a dolt! She deserved brutal honesty. Not brutal for her, of course. Brutal for him. For if he laid out the facts as he now understood them, Miss Elizabeth was far more than tolerable. The error was completely his.

Although it would be possible for her to blend in with a crowd, one look at the lively sparkle in her eye would capture any man's attention, making her stand out as unique. Her figure was light and pleasing. Her dark brown hair revealed ribbons of gold in the candlelight. Her skin reflected her vibrant good health. What kept his attention was the sharpness of her mind. She was not easily intimidated. He valued that in a woman.

His mother appeared frail upon first appearance. Yet, the strength of Lady Anne's will was renowned at Pemberley. With a deft hand, she ruled the household. Her compassion showed his father how grace had more force than iron.

He missed her almost as much at twenty-seven as he had when he was twelve, although for different reasons. Then, he suffered the loss of his source of comfort. He regretted not having her guide him during those important years when a young man discovered that a girl is far more than a bother. His mother would know the sort of lady who would be his true partner, one who would, as Richard suggested, delight his days and pleasure him at night, someone who filled his heart and shared his trials.

Nonetheless, his mother was not there to guide him in knowing whom he could trust. Was Miss Elizabeth Bennet who she appeared to be, or were driving forces outside her control pushing her to become someone he should flee from? He could hardly know.

* * *

JANE ENJOYED the repast provided by the Bingleys, which left Elizabeth with no excuse to avoid joining the others in the drawing room. She would not have minded conversing with Mr. Bingley. Even Mr. Hurst had the potential to be a good subject for sketching characters. Miss Bingley and Mrs. Hurst's mission seemed to be a competition to see who could offer the most painful insult cloaked under the guise of polite conversation.

Elizabeth wanted to smirk. Kitty and Lydia began sharpening their tongues as they waited impatiently to enter society. Insults flew across the dining table at Longbourn without restraint. Her father laughed at his youngest daughters while her mother ignored them. Verbal darts and arrows glanced off the shield Elizabeth kept around her heart. Miss Bingley and Mrs. Hurst's venom meant nothing to her.

Then, there was Mr. Darcy. As a complex character, he was far more challenging to sketch. She had yet to take the measure of the man. Perhaps tonight would be her opportunity. At the least, it would keep her from falling into the pit of ennui. At best, she could sharpen her verbal skills. She did enjoy a lively riposte.

As expected, she was barely seated before the volley began.

Miss Bingley smoothed the silk fabric over her knees. "Eliza Bennet, did your mother send no other gowns for you? I believe we saw you in the same garment as this morning."

"You are kind to be concerned, Miss Bingley. To answer your query: my mother's primary concern was with Jane, as it should be. She knows I am here for my sister's care rather than to entertain or be entertained."

"Hmm. How is dear Jane?"

"She has improved enough that I hope we may return to Longbourn in the morning."

Mr. Bingley spoke up. "Tomorrow? Surely not. The cold November air she would suffer in the carriage could worsen her ailment. No, I will not hear of it."

"Charles!" Miss Bingley said, "If Miss Eliza needs to return to her family, she is best served if we make arrangements now."

"Pray, reconsider," Mr. Bingley pleaded. "An illness can turn bad quickly. I would not want it to be due to a mistaken view that you are not wanted here. Think of Netherfield Park as your home for as long as needed."

"I thank you, sir." Elizabeth genuinely appreciated the gentleman's caution and care. His younger sister, on the other hand, wanted them gone. "Are you enjoying your stay in Hertfordshire?"

"I am delighted with the shire," Mr. Bingley enthused. "There is so much to see and do in managing an estate. Yet, it is the people who draw me. Why, the welcome from my neighbors gave me a sense of belonging. Since the death of our parents five years prior, the four of us have gone from one relative to another. To be in one place where we can settle is a goal I have long cherished."

What a pleasant man!

"How delightful!" Elizabeth smiled at her host. "I cannot imagine living anywhere else or spending a length of time elsewhere."

Mr. Darcy cleared his throat. "Is that true, Miss Elizabeth? For I distinctly recall that you, at one time, intended to sail the Amazon to the Andes Mountains of Peru."

She was stunned. How could he possibly have known of her youthful pursuits? Had someone told him? Only Jane and the Lucases knew of her aborted attempt. She had not even told her father of her failed attempt to find the Inca gold.

"Pray, tell me, sir. How did you obtain this information?"

"I was there."

"You were where?"

Miss Bingley loudly whispered, "Scandalous!"

Mrs. Hurst nodded her agreement.

The corner of Mr. Darcy's eyes tightened as his lips broke into a smile. *My goodness!* He was handsome as the Devil when his face softened.

"My father and I journeyed to Meryton fourteen years ago. Since he was busy conferring with a local gentleman, likely about a map, I strolled to the river. Peering over the bridge, I watched the *HMS Voyager* make her maiden voyage."

Her mouth dropped open. "That was *you*?"

"Yes, it was me."

"But…" She gasped. "I remember you now. I so wanted you to be part of my crew because you were tall and had a pistol. I deeply regretted your departure. However, if I recall correctly, you had responsibilities, did you not?"

"I did," he easily admitted. "In truth, I had forgotten those brief moments by the river until the night of my arrival. Since I was never told your surname, I was not certain the captain was you."

"Captain?" Mr. Bingley leaned closer. "You were the captain of a ship?"

She laughed. "Not at all. It was a tossed-together raft of dubious *floatability* that never made it past the first bend in the river. Mr. Darcy witnessed what must have been the shortest sailing journey in British history. The Admiralty has nothing to gain or fear from me."

"How quaint." Miss Bingley and Mrs. Hurst snickered.

"Ah, but she is not telling you she had a map."

Mr. Darcy was clearly teasing her. She wondered at his motive.

"Copied and drawn by a newly turned seven-year-old girl." She mused. "I could not have found my way to the Thames since I neglected to draw that portion from my father's map. I was doomed to failure before I began."

"What a terrific tale, Miss Elizabeth." Mr. Bingley slapped his knee. "You are a brave soul to make the attempt. Tell me, if you had sunk, do you swim?"

"I do." She turned the tables and asked, "Do you?"

He shook his head. "Unfortunately, none in my family ever learned. My father and grandfather worked all hours of daylight six days a week. Sunday after services, there was always too much to do. The boys in our town spent more time on horseback or in the pubs. Besides, being from the north, the water never seemed to warm enough for my fair skin."

"Charles, Mr. Darcy is also from the North, yet I imagine he swims quite skillfully, like everything else he does."

As a compliment, it fell flat. Instead of his chest swelling at her praise, the man paled.

"I no longer swim."

His hands fisted.

To ease the stifling air at the turn of conversation, Elizabeth said, "Sir, you will be pleased to know that I never again attempted to find the Amazon."

His lips barely moved.

"Instead, I found a paper in Papa's library about the expedition of Meriwether Lewis and William Clark across America."

Mr. Darcy straightened in his chair. "The Corps of Discovery."

Mr. Bingley said, "I know about this. At Eton, most students were fascinated with the idea of traversing a whole continent of newly discovered territory. We read as much as we could find about Indians and bears. Our history instructor challenged us to learn about Captain James Cook and his exploration since both parties sailed the mighty Columbia River. It fascinated me. Now, to learn that a lady of my acquaintance has that same adventurous blood in her veins is exciting."

Miss Bingley snorted. "I would not say 'exciting,' Charles, since everyone knows a woman's place is in the home."

"Or in the shops on Bond Street," Mr. Hurst rebutted, causing Elizabeth to hide her smile behind her fingers.

When she looked up, Mr. Darcy was doing the same. *What was happening? Mr. Darcy has a sense of humor?* She would never have guessed.

Intending to discover if it was an anomaly, Elizabeth asked, "Mr. Bingley, had you gentlemen been tasked to venture into the unknown, what would be the first item you would choose to pack?"

Mr. Bingley answered right away. "Without a doubt, the most important item would be a map. I would search until I found one with detailed descriptions of what to expect."

Pressing her lips together firmly, she glanced at Mr. Darcy.

"Bingley, if only that were possible. A corps of discovery would be the ones making a map since there would not be one available." To Elizabeth, he said, "You have asked a difficult question. To buy me time to consider my answer, I might ask Miss Bingley what she would take."

"Me?" Her hand flew to her chest, pleasure at being asked first, lighting her features. "Why, I would wait to see what you took, sir. Then I would do the same or consider something that would be a complement." After a moment, she added, "My brother-in-law would want a flask of brandy. Louisa would likely take a piece of lace she is reworking."

"I would not!" Her sister had a mind of her own. "I would take *Mysteries of Udolpho*. With a journey of that length, I might finish the book."

Elizabeth chuckled.

Mr. Hurst offered, "I would take my best rifle with plenty of shot. That way, we would have plenty of game to cook over a fire."

"How would you start the fire?" Mr. Bingley asked.

"Well, I guess I would hope you packed your flint and a knife, Bingley."

"That was my choice," Mr. Darcy said. "Without fire, we could not cook or get warm during the cold." He looked directly at Elizabeth. "What of you? Since you have the most experience planning a grand adventure, what would you pack first?"

Elizabeth had been considering her choice as the others

spoke. Therefore, she replied, "I would take a warm quilt to lay on during the heat of summer and wrap myself in during the winter months."

Mr. Bingley clapped. "Well done, all. Between the six of us, we could sustain ourselves for the journey. Two years it took Lewis and Clark. Reports mentioned that they had Indian troubles. Yet, their greatest challenge was the weather."

Elizabeth wondered aloud, "Would you have gone?"

"Me?" Bingley pointed to his chest. "Yes, I believe I would if the opportunity had arisen. As a fifteen-year-old lad, in the year they departed, with more money than sense, I would have needed help to consider the needs of the journey responsibly, but I would have gone. What of you, Darcy? Would you have gone?"

"I was already at Cambridge when I first heard about the Corps of Discovery. Like you, a large group of us read every report we could get our hands upon." He paused. "Yes, even knowing my responsibilities to my family, I would have considered the greater good of helping to open new land to those in need. I would have gone."

"I would have as well," Elizabeth murmured.

"Well, I would have remained in London, where I would be surrounded by people of fashion." Caroline Bingley stated. "Why should I spend time with those American ruffians? For sure, it likely would be worse than being in Hertfordshire. *Savages!*"

"Miss Elizabeth." Mr. Darcy diverted his attention away from Miss Bingley. "At Lucas Lodge, you mentioned you had news about the two small boys we saw outside the bookstore."

He remembered. She was surprised.

"Yes, sir. Miss Lucas and I happened upon them when they were with Mr. Ralph Simms. Mr. Simms explained that they must have been from a distant relative since the ships' captain delivered them to his skiff when last he was at the waterfront on the Thames. He claimed he was not much for caring for children, but he supposed they could help him around his cottage once they grew."

"A dismal prospect." Mr. Bingley observed. "I sympathize with their plight."

As was typical, Miss Bingley also had an opinion. "Of course, we must feel sorry for the inequities suffered by orphans, but, at the same time, we must take care of our own needs before we can assist others. Is that not so, Mr. Darcy?"

The muscle in the man's cheek flexed. "In case you have forgotten, Miss Bingley, with both my parents deceased, I am an orphan, as are you and your siblings. Would you insist that others ignore the monumental loss we feel? I cannot support your opinion."

"Well, yes, of course, we are orphaned. However, I was thinking of poor orphans. None of us are lacking."

"I would sooner have my mother back than the halls of Pemberley."

The conversation had turned into uncharted territory for Elizabeth. Uncomfortable being blessed with the continued existence of two frustrating parents while the others had none, she chose to excuse herself from their company.

"I beg your pardon. I must see to my sister."

As she ascended the staircase, Elizabeth considered how her life would be different without her parents. The prospect was distressing.

CHAPTER 10

The next morning, Elizabeth shared the conversation with Jane.

"How funny that was Mr. Darcy by the river. I would never have guessed." Jane chuckled, which led to a coughing fit. Once she could swallow the cool water Elizabeth offered, she said, "I only remember that he was tall, and he tried to come to your rescue."

"My hero!" Elizabeth pretended to swoon.

"Do not make light of this, Lizzy. His response was honest and true since he had no time to consider alternatives. I was afraid for you. We were strangers. He was under no obligation to help us. Nevertheless, his instinct was to save you. He had no idea the river was shallow where you landed. He risked his own safety. Lizzy, I am pleased, for I think better of him."

"You think better of everyone." Elizabeth's reply was automatic. Yet, Jane was correct. Young Mr. Darcy was pleasant during the interchange. More importantly, he did not condemn her for overreaching her abilities. *Who was this man?* Since it was not the first time she wondered, Elizabeth needed to admit that her ability to sketch characters properly was lacking, or he was much more than his occasional grumpiness.

What stood out to her in Mr. Darcy's comments that she had not shared with her sister was that he wished his mother lived. He made no mention of his father. Were they distant from each other? Had his father disappointed his son, or was the son a disappointment to his father? Elizabeth had no way of knowing. She certainly would never ask.

An hour later, Jane was sleeping. Desiring to spend time with her thoughts, Elizabeth again went to the river. The water lapped at the edges, higher on the bank than the day before. If only her worries could be washed away in the current.

A part of Elizabeth felt old and worn from anxiety about her future and her family. Another part felt young and ignorant. She scoffed. Who was she to believe she was intelligent when she lived unaware of her father's true nature and completely misjudged a man she admired?

She admired Mr. Darcy? Finally admitting the truth, Elizabeth realized that his nature was a perfect foil for her own. In fundamentals, they agreed.

"Miss Elizabeth, I beg you to take care. If the riverbank eroded, you would be in danger."

Without turning, she answered, "Would you come to my aid as you attempted those many years ago?"

Mr. Darcy stepped alongside her. "I will be at ease only when you step back."

Not wanting to increase his distress, she did as he asked.

"I am curious, Mr. Darcy. You said last night that you no longer swim. Did you still swim when you stopped in Meryton?"

"No. There was an accident when I was at Eton. My mother loved to paint a small waterfall in one of Pemberley's streams. She wanted privacy since she enjoyed removing her shoes to dip her toes into the water. She slipped. There was no one to rescue her. I have not been into a river or stream since."

His tale was heartbreaking. "I am sorry to hear it. This makes your attempt to rescue me from the wreckage of the *HMS Voyager* much more poignant. I apologize for causing you fear."

His slight smile reassured her that he bore no resentment.

"Since then, there have been other instances where I lost or almost lost close family around water. I prefer caution now."

"Which is understandable," she reassured him.

"Miss Elizabeth, are you aware a pond is growing behind a dam on Longbourn's property?"

"I am. I believed it to be dangerous. When I asked my father about it, his reply was indifference. I lack power to force a change."

His lips pressed together before he spoke. "I was wondering if you could recommend an approach that might move your father to reconsider his decision to leave the pond unmolested. The long days and nights of rainfall will put a load against the dam that, if not relieved, could cause damage beyond our imaginations. I would hate to see this happen to those who live downriver. They are likely unaware of the danger."

She finally understood. Mr. Darcy cared for others, even strangers, to the point that he acted on their behalf. He was not after glory or prestige since his efforts would be, for the most part, unknown.

Elizabeth also knew that to keep silent on the matter of the dam would mean that she would bear community responsibility. She needed to speak with her father.

"If you would ask Mr. Bingley to arrange our return after

services this morning, I will see what I can do. Papa is not mean. He is merely distracted by something that weighs heavily upon him."

"My coach will be ready for you and your sister when you are prepared to leave. Once you have spoken to your father, please message my valet, Parker, through your housekeeper. This way, I will know how soon we can try to mitigate the danger. Know that Bingley and I will bear the cost."

Heat flooded her cheeks. Did the residents of Netherfield Park know their situation? *How embarrassing!* She understood his character clearly for the first time as if a veil covering her eyes was removed. Her admiration for Mr. Darcy was such that she saw him far differently than she had at the assembly. He was a good man, responsible to his core. He offered kindness to strangers. He towered over her yet was not threatening in the slightest. When she stood next to him, she felt delicate and strong at the same time.

Inside, she sighed. Even if she had the means to attract such a man, her father's actions would chase him away. Something must be done! She was determined. She was ready to act. The dam was not the only danger to Elizabeth Bennet. If she were not careful, she could begin to fall in love with the stern man from Derbyshire.

* * *

Why had he told her about his mother? What a foolish question…. Because Darcy knew in his heart that she would provide the empathy he needed after the memories Miss Bingley cruelly resurrected.

The difference between the two females was striking. One was wealthy, officious, and patronizing. The other was intelligent, joyous, and kind. One repelled him. The other attracted him to the point he dreamed that she was alone inside the carriage with him, traveling between their London house and Pemberley.

Either he needed to consider the possibilities seriously, or he needed to leave Netherfield Park forever.

As he rubbed his chest, Darcy listed several reasons why Miss Elizabeth Bennet did not qualify to be the next mistress of Pemberley. Despite this, his heart ached for her, seeking her out when he should not.

* * *

Elizabeth and Jane's homecoming at Longbourn was unwelcome. Their mother chastised Jane for departing Mr. Bingley's company without an official attachment to the gentleman. She berated Elizabeth for forcing Jane to exit Netherfield Park prematurely.

"You will see us in the hedgerows, Lizzy, or I am not Mrs. Bennet!"

Elizabeth fumed. It was not her fault that the Bennets' future was threatened. At the same time, she empathized with her mother. To have risen above her birth by marrying a gentleman, bearing him five healthy daughters, and managing the house for a quarter century, Francine Bennet deserved sympathy at her pending loss.

"I need to speak with Papa." Elizabeth stiffened her spine, inhaled deeply, then knocked on his study door.

"Enter only if you are Lizzy come to greet your papa."

Oh, Papa! Why did you choose this path to travel?

"How was Netherfield Park? Have you returned engaged to Mr. Bingley, or has Jane? Or will that other gentleman, the tall, wealthy one, be pounding on my door asking for your hand?"

"No, Papa. Jane and I are as unencumbered now as when we left. You still bear the burden of supporting us."

Elizabeth hated to see that crushed, haunted look settling over her father, yet pretending everything was fine yielded nothing. Now was the time for action.

"Papa, we passed the dam on the way from Netherfield Park. I admit to great fear when the carriage and horses were directly in front of the mass. Water is lapping over the top of the highest log, running down over the roadway. Had even that top log let go, you would have lost two daughters in one fatal blow."

He buried his face in his hands but said nothing.

"Mr. Darcy has promised to bear the cost to see the dam dismantled slowly to avert danger to those downstream. Will you give him permission?"

The sound of her father's hands slapping his desk reverberated around the room.

"Mr. Darcy! Why has he taken it upon himself to interfere in another man's business? He is just like his uncle, Lord Matlock. They have maniacal schemes behind their decisions that strip wealth and dignity from hapless landowners. I will do nothing to support his cause. I have paid enough! I am done!"

Elizabeth was confused. *What was happening?*

"Papa, I do not know what you mean. I know who Lord Matlock is. He is one of the most powerful men in the nation. Who is he to you?" Elizabeth added, "And why are you condemning Mr. Darcy for having him as his uncle? Papa, you do not know him. He is a fair man."

"Fair? How could you say this, Lizzy? The man insulted you personally, proving beyond doubt that he is as lofty-minded as Hugh Fitzwilliam. No, Daughter. If we are to speak of safety, it is not the dam that is the most danger. That family is like inviting a rabid fox into our home as a pet. I will not have it. I will not sacrifice my wife and children anymore. Stay away from this Darcy, Lizzy. I insist."

"But Papa, why are you angry with Lord Matlock?"

"Because, Elizabeth, it was his map I purchased. The whole family are vermin."

"Papa!"

"I did not notice the resemblance the first time Mr. Darcy was in my presence, but now I am convinced it was his father all those years ago who revealed the map to be counterfeit. I will *never* transact business of any sort with that family."

"He is honorable. He seeks our advantage, not his." Elizabeth could not keep herself from defending him.

"If I did not know you better, I would think he has cast a spell over you." Her father fell back into his chair, the anger leeching from him. "I have begun selling my book collections and antique maps. I have already started cataloging them. With your help, we could finish tomorrow. The buyer will be here to make an offer on Tuesday. Hopefully, it will be enough to restore most of Longbourn's accounts."

When his fingers caressed the opened book on his desktop, Elizabeth saw the cost of her father's decision. Her sadness for him collided hard with overwhelming relief. Her spirits lifted with the glimmer of hope.

"And the dam?" she pushed.

His shoulders drooped. His hands quivered.

"I cannot think about it now, Lizzy. I am…I am distracted." Thomas Bennet's gaze was on his books. "Possibly tomorrow, we can discuss potential solutions."

"Thank you, Papa."

She still had many questions. Why was her Papa convinced that Mr. Darcy was like his uncle? *Goodness!* Assuming all family members were the same, how could the vast differences between Jane and Lydia be explained? It was impossible!

Worry plagued her. As was her nature, her solace would not come from being indoors. Deciding that a stroll to the river might restore her aplomb, Elizabeth dressed for the cooler temperatures with thick socks, a long wool coat, gloves, a knitted scarf, and a practical bonnet.

She loved Hertfordshire in late autumn. The tall, aged oaks lining the pathway were dressed in warm shades of gold, green, and orange. Wood smoke from the tenant cottages filled the air. Migrating birds flew in formation to their southern destinations.

When she reached the fork in the road, Elizabeth stopped at the edge of the stone bridge. The angry water rushed below her, swirling quickly away from the riverbanks and crashing over the rocks below. Bits of grass and sticks danced on the crests of waves as the water rose and fell. It was normally a peaceful scene. Today it was not.

From behind her, she could hear boyish chatter. Then she could hear it from under the bridge.

Her heart almost stopped when an old skiff with little Jake and Johnny, the boys who wanted a dog, came out from the other side of the bridge. One was seated at the front, his fingers clutching the sides. The other was on the bench seat that split across the middle, his hands gripping the wooden plank.

"Jake! Johnny! What are you about?" Elizabeth hurried from the bridge to the path that ran alongside. She knew from her distant youth that the upcoming bend was treacherous.

As soon as she saw their faces, Elizabeth recognized terror. Tears streaked both Jake's and Johnny's cheeks. Johnny's mouth was open to scream, but no sound came out.

"Jake!" Ripping her scarf and bonnet off, she pulled at the buttons of her coat. When her fingers fumbled from the thickness of her gloves, she stripped them off before dropping her coat to the ground. She increased her speed.

"Help me!" Johnny whimpered as Jake commanded his brother to hold fast.

She could barely hear the words over the pounding of her own heart and the noise of the river.

Quickly passing the area where she sat watching the sinking of her own vessel those many years ago, she lifted her skirt in her fists and leaped over a fallen log. With only seconds to lose, Elizabeth considered her options. The speed and size of the boat was too much for her to grab it safely as it passed. If it grounded on the bend, she might be able to snatch at least one of the boys to safety at the last minute. The other would be in grave danger.

"Help me! Please, help me!" Jake's voice gained volume with each plea.

"Hang on but be prepared to jump."

Water can be a wicked foe. Not three feet from the boat finally running aground, an eddy turned the bow downriver. Elizabeth lost the opportunity to get the boys to safety. Her next chance would be another stone footbridge halfway to Netherfield's main house. She would never be able to run fast enough to make it in time. When the boat slowed and the stern headed toward her, she did the only thing she could do...she jumped, landing half in and half out of the boat, her shins above her boots catching on the hull, her skirt dragging in the water. Using the wooden seat, Elizabeth pulled herself inside.

Immediately, she noticed that the oars were gone.

Reaching forward, she pulled the lad back to the seat across the middle of the vessel. With a child on each side of her, she felt more stable.

Screaming at the top of her lungs, she yelled, "Help! Help us, please!"

Little Johnny's arms shot around her waist as the skiff rocked and spun. Soon after, so did Jake's.

J. DAWN KING

"I'm afraid," Jake admitted.

She felt the same fear, though she did not say it aloud.

Elizabeth hated the loss of control. For a certainty, she realized that lacking power for her future was that exact complaint that had driven her from Longbourn. Yet, this was so much more terrifying than the potential of losing a home. The threat to their very lives was imminent.

Elizabeth hugged the boys tightly to her side. They were freezing. She felt cold dampness crawling through her gown. "Can you swim?"

Johnny buried his nose in her shoulder. Jake said, "Not very well. Well, actually, no. My papa was going to teach me, but he didn't get to 'fore he died. Bek..ah, I mean, Johnny didn't like the water."

"I see." Elizabeth studied both sides of the river. They were almost at the last of Longbourn's fields on her right. Soon, they would be at the border of Mr. Bingley's property. Was anyone about?

"Help!" she screamed again. This time, the children chimed in.

The debris banged loudly on the sides of the skiff.

At the same time that she noticed a horse and rider approaching them from the Netherfield side, a loud crack and then a roar filled the air. Dirt flew into the sky as a wall of water, downed trees, and massive boulders came toward them. Holding Jake and Johnny tighter, she prayed for help just before her world went dark.

* * *

TIRED OF MISS BINGLEY'S complaints, tired of Bingley's raptures over Miss Bennet's beauty, and tired of other men's indolence (in particular, Mr. Thomas Bennet, master of Longbourn), Darcy called for a horse to be readied. Using the excuse that he wanted to spend time alone to consider a weighty decision, he refused Bingley's offer to accompany him. Instead, he surveyed the property as he rode high above the river, prioritizing his actions if the land belonged to him.

First, he would drain that pond.

He knew the power of an errant river. He shook his head at Mr. Bennet's foolhardiness.

From a safe distance, he estimated the volume of water that would release if the dam collapsed. The pond looked approximately one hundred feet by three hundred feet, almost three-quarters of an acre. Judging by the pile of debris, the height from the bottom of the dam to the top was about eight feet, narrowing at the back to less than a few inches. Using calculations he had learned at university, Darcy guessed nearly one million gallons of water would gush from the pond, stripping acres of valuable topsoil while leaving worthless mud behind.

Instinctively backing his horse away from the water, Darcy worried for the strangers who lived in the path of potential disaster. If they were fortunate, the rains would hold off until some of the pond's contents could be diverted into the bottomlands slowly enough that most of the water would be absorbed into the ground or channeled to the river Lea.

Already the river overflowed the banks, trickling into the roadway. His horse pulled against the bit away from the embankment. Darcy did not blame her. How eerie to have so much water on either side of him. He hated it, his worst enemy, his most feared scenario.

Squeezing his thighs, Darcy directed the horse toward a knoll where he could see down into the pond. The water was murky and still.

The mare nickered, shifting her weight to the side. When Darcy turned his head to see what might have disturbed the animal, a plaintive cry hit him. Somewhere nearby, a woman was in distress.

With horror, he saw a skiff tossed and turned by the tumult in the river. At the same time, a sound like a dozen rifles firing and the appearance of a large wave rippling across the pond woke him to danger.

Good lord! A woman and children were in the boat headed to the exact spot where the dam was breaking apart. Pulling on the reins, Darcy gave the mare a sharp kick, setting the animal in motion. Racing back to the bridleway, he ran the horse, keeping the skiff within sight. He recognized her and the boys at the same time that he realized he would never reach the next bend in time. Miss Elizabeth? *Blast!* The boys had to be the children from outside the bookshop. *How had...? Why was she on a skiff with these children...?*

He rode like a battalion of Napoleon's soldiers were chasing him. "Miss Bennet!" he yelled.

There was no time to get assistance. If Darcy could not get them out of the boat and the river, they would never...oh, *God in heaven!* A log slammed into the side of the skiff, lifting the stern until the bow dove under water tossing its occupants out like unwanted rag dolls.

"Miss Elizabeth!" he yelled until his throat hurt. Spying a bridge in the distance, Darcy urged the horse on.

Over the pounding of the hooves, he could hear the dam breaking apart behind them. If he did not hurry, the whole mass would give way, and there would be no rescuing the three nor saving anyone else in the water's path.

Reaching the stone bridge, he leapt from the horse.

Somehow, amidst the debris, Miss Elizabeth clutched one of the tree limbs with one arm, and the other held the boys to her chest.

Darcy needed a rope. Glancing about, he saw nothing to help him.

Stripping off his great coat and hat, he toed the heel of his boot. Only one hit the ground before he discerned he was out of time. Damn his fears!

His heart pounded, threatening to explode from his chest. Sweat poured down his forehead into his eyes, the sting a reminder of everything wrong that could happen.

He gulped.

The river made a slight turn before it reached the bridge. If the tree Elizabeth held navigated the bend successfully, they would be only a few feet from the bank when they passed. Unfortunately, the water forced them to the middle of the widening water. Darcy's only option was to jump.

He hated the water, but he admired…he deeply admired her.

Tamping down his rising panic, he leapt from the bridge and plunged into the cold, churning water below.

CHAPTER 11

Waves of freezing water pressed at her back as branches and gravel struck her from every angle. Elizabeth swiped the mud from her eyes with the back of her hand. Johnny's head crashed into her chin, causing her to see stars where the gray sky had been. As the flooding river churned, the log they held bounced and twisted. Her grip was strong enough to hold the small boys above water with one arm so she could hang onto the log with the other.

Her skirt tangled around her legs. Her walking boots filled, acting as weights determined to pull them all under.

Above the roar of the water, she heard a voice calling her. Elizabeth glanced up in time to see a man jumping from the bridge right in the path of their errant log. It was…it was… *Mr. Darcy? Was he mad?*

Desperately searching the surface for him to reappear, relief almost weakened her at seeing his flailing arms when he surfaced. She yelled, "Mr. Darcy!" She tightened her grip as she repeated his name until he saw them.

Just before he reached them, Elizabeth felt the log begin to roll. Fear nearly overwhelmed her that she might lose hold of the boys. She was a good swimmer. Her legs were strong. But two lads hanging around her neck threatened her physical ability. Without a doubt, she knew she must hang on to the tree limb to keep afloat. But as the log started to roll and take them under, that was no longer an option. Pushing away with all her strength, Elizabeth spun onto her back, kicking her legs rapidly. Both children screamed, their skinny arms squeezing her neck until breathing became almost impossible.

Was she going to die? Was this her end?

Water was everywhere; choking, Elizabeth struggled to breathe.

With conviction, she tightened her arms around the children, then snapped her legs together, thrusting them toward the embankment. Hoping Mr. Darcy was safe, she kicked in a steady rhythm until she felt she had gained some control. Mud and other debris battered her side.

Exhaling quickly, she took another deep breath when something pulled at one of the boys. Her arm tightened. She would not….

"Let me have him."

Mr. Darcy. She felt his hand on her back as the other pulled a boy away. Immediately, she felt light enough to make better progress.

With a swift move, Mr. Darcy pushed her toward the embankment. Shifting the lad more comfortably against her chest, she assured him, "All will be well. Help has arrived." Wild-eyed, Johnny only nodded.

Not once did Mr. Darcy let go of her arm, his grip tightening amidst the current of churning debris. With his assistance, Elizabeth imagined they might survive this ordeal. In what shape they would be, she could not guess.

* * *

Blast! The freezing depths robbed Darcy of breath.

Struggling against the current, he finally surfaced, gasping for air. Swirling his arms in the water, his right hand struck the log Elizabeth had held onto. *Where is she?*

Swiping the water from his eyes, he saw her, face pale and bloodied. He pulled himself through the water until he clasped Elizabeth's arm.

Wrenching one of the children away from her, Darcy settled the boy tighter against his chest.

"Hold on. I have you," Darcy said over the sound of the flood.

They needed to get to shore, out of the water, and away from all the heavy debris. Wood and rock might crush them. He worried if they did not get out of the river soon, the cold would weaken him, and how could he save them then?

The current carried them further away from the stone bridge. The banks were steep and bare. There was nothing with which he could pull them out of the water. Seeing the fear on the lad's face, Darcy said, "Hang on. Miss Bennet has your brother. And I have Miss Bennet."

"Mr. Darcy." Her anguished voice jolted him out of his thoughts. "The boat…"

He glanced at Miss Elizabeth before his eyes followed hers. The skiff was twisting and bucking along with the current.

"Grab my collar, Elizabeth. I need to shift him between us. I must let go of your arm."

Before the words were out of his mouth, she did as he asked. He prayed the buttons of his morning coat would hold. With a powerful kick, Darcy reached the wooden hull. Sweeping his right arm behind him, he drew the others close. He grabbed one of the gunnels as he lifted one boy and then the next into the boat. His buckskin trousers were heavy. His lone Hessian filled to the brim. At some point, he lost the wool sock on his left foot.

The two small children could not ballast the skiff, and Darcy feared his weight would upset the boat, tossing them back into the water when he attempted to pull himself aboard.

Miss Elizabeth must have determined the same because she began moving hand over hand around the stern. Once she reached the other side, she loudly counted to three and pulled herself up, her chest resting on the gunnels as ballast. Darcy lifted himself up and over, then reached for her hands, dragging her into the boat.

The skiff had lost its oars and had no other means to steer. He could feel Elizabeth's eyes on him as he surveyed their situation. A log hit aft, spinning their tiny vessel around until they raced backward down the river.

Rough edges caught his morning coat and waistcoat and destroyed the fabric of her gown. Reaching behind the lads, Darcy wrapped his hand around her ribcage, pulling everyone close.

"Boys!" Elizabeth said, her teeth chattering. "Let us look for a safe place to land."

Jake nodded at her suggestion. Johnny did not. His immediate response was, "I want to go home."

Elizabeth reached around Jake to stroke Johnny's cheek. "I want the same."

* * *

ELIZABETH AND DARCY pulled the lads onto their laps. Moving closer to the center of the boat, they immediately felt more stable. There was nothing she could do to keep from shivering. The cold sank through her skin to her bones. If they survived this ordeal, she feared she would never be warm again. With one arm around Jake, she boldly wrapped the other around the man huddled next to her for warmth. His back was firm under the soft weave of his coat. Gratefully, he did not flinch at her touch.

She spoke over the water slapping against the hull. "I have never walked beyond Netherfield Park, so I am not certain where this meets the river Lea. We must be close, though." She rubbed Jake's back in a slow circular motion.

Mr. Darcy nodded. "We need to get to shelter, get dry. It appears that only the top portion of the dam was all that gave way. Should the rest become unstable, our situation and that of others in the area will be perilous."

Unspoken fears gripped her. How far from Longbourn had they traveled already? As it was, there was nothing of her surroundings that she recognized. Distant farmhouses dotted the landscape on both sides of the river.

"Help! Help us!" The occupants of the boat yelled to no avail. Oblivious to anything but their own emergencies, people frantically attempted to keep the flood waters from their homes and fields.

A steady starboard wind hit, and their situation became more hazardous with every passing second. Darcy caught her attention, his brows furrowed. Even though their situation was dire, Elizabeth drew comfort from his presence.

His eyes scoured the riverbanks as she considered ways to ease the children's fears.

Just then, they heard a dog bark, startling them all. The animal running across the field was one of the most long-legged creatures Elizabeth had ever seen. As it drew closer to the water, the wiry gray and brown dog stopped and barked loudly.

"Boys, look at that dog. Would you like a dog like that?"

Jake said, "I want a black dog with white spots."

She ruffled Johnny's wet curls, wondering about his

crudely chopped hair. "And you? Would you want a spotted dog?"

"Yes," was the muffled reply, the boy burying his face in Darcy's chest.

The boat crested one wave and plunged through another. "What would you call him?"

"Spot!" Jake shouted. "I'd call him Spotty when I need to yell at him and plain old Spot when I don't."

Grinning at the boy, she asked Johnny the same.

"I'd call him Spot too."

"Well then." Elizabeth nodded. "If we find a dog like that, we'll call him Spot."

CHAPTER 12

Darcy's worry grew as no living soul acknowledged their presence. When it came to survival, they were on their own. The air was frigid, and they were soaked. There was no food or drinkable water in sight. Who knew where they would finally come to rest?

He rubbed his hands over the boy's arms and legs, even squeezing the lad's bare toes into his palms. Elizabeth did the same to the other child. Yet, through all their distress, not one word of complaint had come from any of them.

The child on his lap peered up at him through heavy lashes, his rich chocolate eyes as large and luminous as Elizabeth's. Peering closer, Darcy studied the boy's face: dark brown brows perfectly arched, high cheekbones, elfin chin.

Darcy whispered, "Is your name really Johnny?"

"Bekah. I am Rebekah," the child admitted, causing everything to fall into place.

A girl! A little girl in need of a hero. "How old are you?" Darcy asked.

"Five. Me and Jake is twins. I was born first. He was second. He's bigger than me."

"A girl!" Elizabeth smiled. "But you told us you were Johnny?"

"Mama said it was safer to be a boy."

"I see." Elizabeth glanced at him.

He understood. The world was not always a secure place.

The children said no more. Darcy's protective instincts had been stirred the instant he saw them in the boat. Nevertheless, knowing the little one was a girl brought mental images of his sister when she was that age. His greatest desire was to be her protector, her knight in shining armor. He failed his sister at Ramsgate. He vowed to do all within his power to aid little Rebekah, her brother, and Miss Elizabeth.

Without thought, the fingers of his left hand unfastened the buttons of his coat.

"Sir, you also need warmth." Elizabeth protested.

"Not at the expense of these children."

Elizabeth helped him draw the wet garment off. Immediately, the November wind cut through the linen on his arms and neck.

After wringing out the water, Elizabeth helped tuck his coat around the children. His heart sank when a drop of rain landed on the bridge of his nose. Another drop followed. Turning toward Elizabeth, he drew her in until they touched from head to toe. Leaning over, in vain, he tried to shelter the others from the downpour.

* * *

THROUGH HER FEARS, Elizabeth's admiration for Mr. Darcy grew. She was grateful for the courage it took to jump into the river.

The skiff skipped unpredictably over the water as the wind picked up and the rain poured. At the first sharp bend, the bow hit the riverbank hard before bouncing back into the swift current. The same happened at the second bend.

A dark shadow loomed in front of them.

"What is…?" Elizabeth could not keep her voice from rising.

At her words, Darcy looked up.

"Down! *Blast!* Get down." He pushed Elizabeth and the children roughly to the deck of the boat. "Lay as flat as possible."

The wood scraped her hands and her cheeks. Rolling to her back, she pulled the children over her, so their faces were out of the water pooling at the bottom of the boat. Darcy barely made it down before they passed under a stone bridge. It was a tight fit, the top of the hull scraping rock as it passed below. Elizabeth felt Darcy's body jerk and knew he had not escaped injury.

She reached behind him, and the stones instantly scraped the flesh from her knuckles. What they had done to Darcy was unimaginable.

The poor man!

Bemoaning his injuries, Elizabeth admitted to herself that she was extremely grateful he was in the boat with them. Never could she have dragged the children into the skiff on her own. Nor could she have made it inside without pulling the vessel over.

As they emerged from under the bridge, she realized they would never have survived without Darcy. He was their hero. She shuddered. What if…no, she could not think that way. Darcy sacrificed his health and life to save them. She would not question his motive; she would only be thankful for his kindness.

"Mister…" a tiny voice said. "You are laying on me crooked. Can we sit up now?"

Darcy groaned. Reaching forward, he pulled each child

next to him before extending his arm for her. Without hesitation, she placed her hand in his.

Lifting the coat from the deck, Elizabeth wrung the water before placing it back around the children. Despite its dampness, the garment protected them from the wind.

She doubted that Darcy wanted attention to his injury, so she distracted Jake and Rebekah until they did not notice the palm of her hand moving over his back. He could not keep himself from wincing when she lightly brushed the area of his shoulder. His shredded shirt flapped in the wind. Holding the fabric in place, she pressed it into his injury to staunch the bleeding.

"Are we going to die like our papa?" Jake asked. "I'm scared. I wanna go home."

Elizabeth wanted to cry, too, until she realized how smoothly the skiff moved with the river. Looking back, it seemed the bridge caught the bulk of the debris.

Darcy pulled the boy close. "Let me tell you about one of the bravest men I know. His name is Colonel Richard Fitzwilliam. Before I came to Hertfordshire, he came to my house to inform me that he would soon set sail to fight for the safety of the four of us. Do you know, he was not afraid, not at all."

"Is he a soldier? Does he have a horse?" Jake asked, his eyes glued to Darcy.

"He has a cavalry horse named Excalibur, a massive black gelding as fierce in battle as is Richard."

"I bet he's not afraid of nothing." The children hung on his every word.

Darcy smiled. "You would be wrong, Jake, because as fierce as my cousin and his horse are, they are both terribly afraid of snakes."

"I don't mind snakes," Jake said.

Teeth chattering, Rebekah added, "I do."

"I do too." Elizabeth had never been fond of the creatures, so her immediate sympathy was with the colonel.

As Mr. Darcy continued his tale, she scanned the upcoming riverbanks for a safe place to land. She caught his eyes doing the same.

"Well, let me tell you what Colonel Fitzwilliam told me when he returned to England after fighting several battles." Darcy sobered. "The enemy surrounded Richard's battalion. They were almost out of ammunition, and all they had were bayonets and their swords. Napoleon's troops had backed them into a walled canyon where it looked like there was no escape."

"Did he make it? Did his horse?" Jake asked.

"Did they?" Rebekah's large eyes widened in wonder.

"Now, imagine you were there. You have fought all day, so weariness has set in. Your arms and legs have lost strength, and your horse is ready to drop. The commander of the French forces taunts you, challenging you to surrender."

"What did he do? Did he give up?" asked Jake.

"Did he die?" whispered Rebekah.

"Richard told the enemy commander that he was not yet done fighting. To a proud man like the French officer, he scoffed at Colonel Fitzwilliam. Exhausted and wanting the fight to end, Richard boldly pulled off his gloves, rode to where the enemy sat on their horses and slapped the commander across the face with the leather, signaling the man that the duel between the two of them would be to the death."

Elizabeth's heart pounded with each word. She knew the story had a good ending since, according to his narrative, Colonel Fitzwilliam had been at the gentleman's house before Mr. Darcy arrived in Hertfordshire. Nonetheless, she was eager to hear the rest of the tale.

"The man accepted." Darcy cleared his throat. "Now, you

should know that Colonel Richard Fitzwilliam is my cousin, my favorite cousin. He is the best of men with a sharp mind and a quick wit. Therefore, when the other man dismounted as Richard had done, my cousin threw down his sword and his empty pistol. As the other officer stood with his fists ready to pummel Richard, my cousin swooped down and grabbed a snake from underneath a rock where it had crawled. Throwing it at the other officer, the man screamed like a baby as he scrambled out of the way."

"I woulda caught the snake and thrown it back," Jake said.

"I wouldn't," said Rebekah.

Elizabeth added, "I would have screamed like a baby too."

Darcy smiled.

She sincerely appreciated his efforts to lighten the mood. He was rugged and manly, and…Elizabeth's heart leapt. She had difficulty swallowing. *This was Mr. Darcy! Good heavens!*

He continued. "The French officer's regiment laughed, as did Richard's soldiers. The commander yelled at his men, mounted his horse, and left, taking his regiment with him. They never came back. If you read the records of the battle in the newspapers, you will see mention of the bravery and courage of one Richard Fitzwilliam. Nothing at all is said of the snake."

"I wanna be brave." Jake almost bounced in his excitement.

"I don't," said Rebekah. "I don't want to touch a snake…ever."

"Me either," Elizabeth agreed.

Darcy looked directly at the children. "The point is that even the bravest of men have fears. Even the most scared of men can act bravely. What you two are doing today is exceedingly courageous. You are with two people you do not know in a boat going who knows where, and you have not complained once. Jake and Rebekah, this is the meaning of bravery. Your parents would be proud of you. I am proud, and I believe that Miss Elizabeth is too."

Part of Elizabeth's heart melted. She wanted to hug him for the hope and valor he instilled in the children and her. *Who was this man?* Their bodies pressed together for warmth, she felt no fear from Mr. Darcy, only relief for his presence and deep respect for his actions. At that second, she knew she had never admired a man as much as Mr. Darcy.

Jake leaned his head back on her shoulder. "Mama said that we might have cousins. Maybe we have a boy cousin for me who likes dogs and snakes and a girl cousin for Bekah who will play dolls with her."

Elizabeth acknowledged the comment and then asked Mr. Darcy, "Sir, is the colonel your only cousin?"

The children gave him their rapt attention as if his answer would give them hope.

"I have several distant cousins on the Darcy side of the family. Richard has an older brother, Viscount Smithton, who is as opposite in character to my honorable cousin as could be. His goal seems to be to bankrupt the earldom. His two younger sisters are elegant ladies of the *ton* whose sole purpose in life seems to be attaining the highest position in the kingdom by marriage. They are silly girls driven by their parents to be the best. My cousin Anne de Bourgh is sickly."

She had to ask. "Your mother's family is Fitzwilliam? Is that where you got your name, then?"

He nodded. "Yes. My father desired to name me after a favorite tutor who opened his eyes to the value of books at a young age. The man died not two weeks before my birth. To honor him, Father chose the name Archibald. Mother balked, gaining her way. I am forever grateful."

Elizabeth barely contained herself. Her conversation with Charlotte when she produced the sobriquet Arrogant Archibald Arse-y was still fresh.

Gratefully, Jake said, "I'm hungry, and I'm cold. If the colonel were here, he would catch the boat and take me to Pennsylvania, where I can see Max, our dog."

Rebekah nodded. "I wanna see Max. And I want my dolly, my bed, the biscuits Mama used to make, our garden, and my papa." Looking down at her lap, she whispered, "And I have to…ah, you know."

There was nowhere in the boat for the sort of privacy Rebekah would require. They needed to be rescued, and they needed it now.

CHAPTER 13

Between the wind, the rain, and the swirling water below, Darcy's concern for their survival increased. Although they had been on the river for less than ten minutes, they were wet and cold, lips blue.

When a cloud burst above them, their situation became even more desperate.

"Look!" Elizabeth pointed toward a low bank.

Sliding Rebekah from his lap, Darcy's first inclination was to kiss Elizabeth for spying the grassy slope first. Instead, he said, "Miss Elizabeth, I shall need the plank we are sitting upon."

Kneeling, Darcy wedged his thigh under the board. As he suspected, the rusty nails easily gave way. Within seconds, he had a rudder. It would take his full strength to control the board underwater.

Leaning over the stern, he held the wooden plank behind them. The muscles in Darcy's upper arms burned like a thousand torches while his lower arms numbed in the cold. The rough wood shredded the skin on his fingertips and palms.

Gritting his teeth, he battled the elements and the demon river until he sensed the skiff turn. Determined, he adjusted the angle until he felt like his arms would rip from their sockets.

The wind carried Elizabeth's voice back to him. "Sir, you did it!"

The skiff shook the moment the boat hit the grassy surface. Tossing the plank aside, he jumped into the water as the current swung the stern around. His feet slid on the muddy bottom, the water lapping at his chest. With all his might, he pushed the skiff forward until Elizabeth and the children disembarked safely onto the grass.

"Come, children. Pull!" All three grabbed the front of the boat. Once he was close enough, he clutched Elizabeth's hand, letting go of the skiff. By the time he reached their side, the vessel was barely visible as it bounced around the next bend. Darcy regretted the loss of the boat. If they did not find immediate shelter, they could have used it temporarily, curling underneath to protect them from the rain. But he was simply not strong enough to hang on against the current.

The fabric of her gown stuck to her legs, hampering Elizabeth's movements. Darcy's single boot slid on the damp earth. For the moment, he wished both feet were bare like the children, who had no difficulty scampering away from the river, their toes digging into the mud.

At the top of the knoll, they slowed to survey their surroundings. The little girl wrapped her arms around his hips, shivering. In the turmoil of reaching land, his morning coat had been left behind in the skiff.

In front of them, he spotted a large shadow that could be a building. Whether it was a barn, a shed, or a residence, he cared not. They needed any shelter they could find.

"Come." Clasping Rebekah's hand, they hurried through

the grass to a narrow pathway. "Jake, hold onto Miss Elizabeth."

As they neared the building, they saw rainwater pouring off its steep-pitched roof and small well-trimmed shrubs bordering the path leading to the door. There was no light in the windows—no welcoming smoke from a fire. Whoever lived in the cottage was not home.

Praying that the occupant was a kindly soul, Darcy lifted the latch, grateful when the door swung open so he could usher the others inside.

The humble cottage was cozy, with drying herbs scenting the air, a colorful quilt covering the bed, and curtains that looked to have been a sunny yellow at one time. The walls were bare. The few pieces of furniture were well-used. Next to the door was a pair of well-worn heavy boots, a bucket, and a broom. Along the wall facing the river was a bench holding another bucket. A massive pan likely used for cleaning dishware had a small towel draped over the edge. A ruffled apron hung from a peg on one side of the window. Against a side wall, a table with two chairs nestled between the bench, a cupboard holding linens, and a stone fireplace. Carefully stacked on the hearth were dry kindling and chunks of wood.

Everything was tidy. The floor was swept, the windows cleaned, and the dust layer on the furniture was thin. Whoever lived there had not been absent for long.

* * *

"Bless whoever lives in this house," Elizabeth muttered. "Do you think the resident is away for a while, or should we expect their immediate return?" Elizabeth asked. She sincerely hoped they were the sort who willingly offered hospitality to strangers.

"I do not know." Darcy opened the cupboard, which turned out to be an armoire. Several men's shirts and a faded day dress filled the narrow space. The drawers held fabric of various sizes and purposes. The only garments were torn shirts that needed mending and trousers that would be several inches too short for Darcy.

Darcy dumped the fabric from the bottom drawer on the bed. Elizabeth sorted through the pieces until she found cotton to dry the children. She separated heavier pieces to wrap them in until they could start a fire. The cottager's shirts would be too small for Darcy. Elizabeth held the gown up to her. The woman who occupied the house was much shorter and rounder than Elizabeth. However, she would make do.

Her cold fingers fumbled with the ties on Rebekah's shirt and pants as Darcy placed the smallest pieces of wood in the fireplace. On the mantelpiece, he found a flint and striker. Within short order, a small welcoming flame danced from the kindling.

"Well done, Mr. Darcy," Elizabeth exclaimed, the children immediately echoing her cheer. She was surprised to see a blush on his cheeks.

When he turned toward the fire, Elizabeth had a clearer view of his injured back. Tiny rivulets of blood seeped from where the rocks had scraped the top layer of skin from his shoulder blade. The area looked like it was on fire.

"Might I tend your wound, sir?" she asked softly.

"Not yet. Some things must be done first." The look he gave her was firm.

Returning her attention to the children, she said, "As soon as we get you out of your wet clothes and the fire grows, you shall be warm to your bones."

Rebekah gasped as her eyes fastened on Mr. Darcy's back. A tear dripped down her cheek. "You are hurt."

Mr. Darcy spun around, dropping the kindling back on the pile.

"Please do not be concerned. I am well, Miss Rebekah. There is nothing to worry about since it is merely a scratch or two. Do not fret, I pray you."

"But it's bleeding."

This caught Jake's attention. "Let me see. I know all about scrapes. My knees have been bloody so many times that my mama said they should be permanently red."

Kneeling on the floor so both children could study the torn skin, Mr. Darcy shrugged. Jake leaned closer. Rebekah's fingers traced the wound.

"Yep. It's scraped, that's for sure. It helps to blow on it." At that, both children sucked their cheeks full of air and then blew three or four times. "There. That should be better."

Elizabeth caught Mr. Darcy's smile before he thanked the twins.

"How fortunate I am for your medical expertise. I do believe my shoulder will be as good as new in no time due to your excellent care."

Jake's chest puffed up while Rebekah shyly grinned.

The interaction further warmed Elizabeth's heart.

Within a few minutes, Mr. Darcy moved the rest of the woodpile to the side, allowing Jake and Rebekah to sit on the hearth. Enjoying the growing flames, Jake wore a red plaid wool shirt with a rip in the elbow, and Rebekah wore a blue cotton shirt with the front pocket hanging off. Unfortunately, they only found five green socks. But it mattered not since the twins were finally getting warm.

"Miss Elizabeth, I beg your pardon for leaving you alone, but I need to bring in water and see if any produce remains in the kitchen garden. I pray that you can keep the firing going and warm yourself as you are able."

Moving to the door, he used his bare toes to try to pry off

his lone boot. After a few attempts, the footwear slid off with a suction noise once his foot was free. Without hesitation, he stripped off his stocking and plunged his wet feet into the boots by the door.

Elizabeth was stunned. His behavior had surprised her at every stage since he jumped into the water. Where she had thought him fastidious before, she knew better now.

With him leaving the house, she felt comfortable removing her boots and setting them by the fire. Her stockings and shift landed in a heap next to the heat too. Quickly, she changed into the day dress their hostess left behind. She draped her wet garments over the two chairs she pulled close to the warmth.

Joining Jake and Rebekah on the hearth, Elizabeth studied them closely. They were handsome children. They looked nothing like Ralph Simms, the lazy fisherman from Meryton. When he removed his cap, Mr. Simms had coal-black hair that stood on end. His face, neck, and the backs of his hands were heavily freckled. His face was round, as was the rest of him.

"Your name is Miss Elizabeth," Jake stated.

"Yes, Jake. I am Miss Elizabeth Bennet. You are Jake Simms."

His eyes darted to her. His chin lifted. "I am not. My name is Jake Stephen Simmons."

"No, it's not," his sister added. "You're Jacob Stephen Simmons, and I'm Rebekah Joy Simmons."

Elizabeth was puzzled. Then why were they with Ralph Simms if they did not share the same last name? "Not Simms?"

Rebekah answered, "I hope he's not our uncle. He is a mean man who doesn't like us at all. He made us sleep on the floor in the corner away from the fire, and we had to beg him for food."

"Yeah, it's why we were running away to America," Jake added.

"Did your mother say that Mr. Ralph Simms was your uncle?"

"Nah." Jake tapped his foot on the floor. "The man what met us at the ship read the letter in my…." He patted his chest, a look of panic on his face. "Oh no! Bekah, we left the tin box at mean Uncle Ralph's." Tears poured from his eyes. "Mama told me not to lose the tin. She made me promise that I would keep it safe."

As soon as the words burst from him, his sister also began to cry. "Jake, you were 'posed to keep it safe. I was 'posed to help you protect that box."

The lad hung his head, his broken heart evident by the pain on his face. Elizabeth reassured him, "I have no doubt that your mother would far rather have you alive than have the box."

Rebekah said, "But you don't understand. Mama put a very 'portant letter inside my papa's special papers. She told us it was for our future or something like that."

Jake nodded as he wiped away his tears. "It's valuable." He lowered his voice, "Really valuable."

"I am terribly sorry you do not have the tin." Elizabeth suggested, "Perhaps after we return to Meryton, we can ask Mr. Darcy to visit Mr. Simms to retrieve the box."

"Can we?"

Elizabeth knew with confidence that the gentleman from Derbyshire would act on behalf of the children. The children may fear Mr. Simms, but Mr. Darcy would not.

* * *

AFTER SCRAPING the boots on the rocks outside the door, Darcy pulled on the handle. The first thing he did when he left the house was to fill the bucket from a barrel filled with rainwater. Careful not to jostle the bucket, he set the container on the floor.

The heat radiating from the fire hit him like a warm welcome from his favorite pup. Elizabeth had hung a large pot from the chimney crane. The wood coals were mottled shades of orange, hissing and snapping.

She hurried to him to remove the buckets from his hands. "Come to the fire, Mr. Darcy, and warm yourself."

"I must bring in more water before I can dry off." Pouring the first bucket into the pot hanging from the iron, he set the other on the bench. "I found a small orchard behind the cottage. Four apple trees held a large crop that easily fell to the ground with one violent shake. The kitchen garden had rows of small cabbages, almost a dozen squash, tall stems of Brussels sprouts, leeks, what looked like onion tops, and carrots. Mounds of potatoes lined the walkway." Dipping the bucket in and out of the river, he had washed away most of the mud from the tubers, the apples, and one small cabbage.

The windows fogged from the steam coming from their wet garments. Darcy turned his eyes away from Elizabeth's shift draped over the chairs. His gaze landed on the children at the hearth. The domesticity warmed his heart as much or more than the heat from the fire.

Emptying the produce into the wash pan, he returned to the rain barrel twice more for water. Elizabeth stood at the bench washing the apples and potatoes.

He asked, "Do you know how to cook?" He hoped she answered in the affirmative since he had no idea how or what to do with the fruit and vegetables other than eat them raw. He was hungry enough to eat kale, something he abhorred.

She shook her head. "I do not." Drying her hands, she pulled the tins from under the bench. Opening them one by one, she first smelled them before putting a bit of whatever was inside on the tip of her tongue. "Nevertheless, I do believe that at least one of us is intelligent enough to figure out the fundamentals." Grinning, she added, "It might be you, sir."

He chuckled. "I was never allowed in the kitchen. My cousin convinced me that flirting with Cook's helper was the best way to have her overlook us pilfering berry scones. It worked for him but did not for me. My cousin laughed as I was soundly scolded for my attempt at thievery. I never dared breach the kitchen or the pantry again. But the vegetables should taste good after being roasted in the hot coals."

Her laughter was musical, easing that little voice in his head that chastised him for sharing an intimate detail of his life that might serve to lower him in her estimation. A Darcy never did or said anything to draw attention to a flaw. His father would have frowned and then reprimanded him later in privacy.

Darcy hesitated. Finally, comprehending need over propriety, he blurted, "There is a privy at the back of the orchard."

Elizabeth nodded. "Yes, I see. Then if you do not mind, I shall take the children immediately." Gaining their attention, she said, "Come, children. We must hurry, or we'll get wet."

Quickly removing their green socks, the twins hurried in front of Elizabeth to the door.

For the first time since the ordeal began, Darcy was alone.

Elizabeth had set out one of the shirts, the trousers, and the last green sock on the bed. Quickly, Darcy changed. Nothing fit, but he was finally getting warm. What he needed was something to heat his insides.

He found a treasure inside a small cupboard next to the kitchen bench. Reaching up, he retrieved a pink teapot with flowers painted on the lid, the handle, and the spout. Beside it were two heavy ceramic mugs. Opening the lid on the smallest tin, he smelled the sweetness of sugar. Another small tin yielded salt, and another contained loose black tea. Dumping some leaves in the teapot, he filled it with water from the hearth. Immediately, the scent of brewing tea filled the air.

His body had taken a beating during their trials in the river. Yet, he was so grateful they were all alive that it mattered not. Contributing his strength toward their survival made him feel a sense of pride unrelated to the Darcy name. Would his father have been pleased with his actions that day, or would he have scoffed at his son endangering himself for three individuals so unrelated to them? Darcy could not know for certain. However, he suspected Gerald Darcy would have never gone close to the water in the first place. He would have ridden away, expecting someone else to come to the rescue.

CHAPTER 14

Quickly returning to the cottage, Elizabeth joined the children by the fire. The outside air was frigid.

The temperature inside was almost humid. Mr. Darcy was at the bench cutting the potatoes into thick slices. Next, he did the same to the apples, cutting the flesh directly away from the core. Scooping a spoonful of fat from one of the tins, he placed an iron pan directly onto the coals closest to the hearth. He dropped the apples into the water.

"Miss Elizabeth, I have done all I can. Pray, use your judgment for how much salt and sugar to add."

The pop and sizzle of the potatoes in the oil filled the room with the lovely smell of cooked pork.

As Jake and Rebekah put their socks back on, they danced in a circle before they spotted the teapot.

"Thank you, Mr. Darcy. I cannot imagine anything finer on a day like today." Elizabeth poured into the two ceramic mugs, adding a pinch of sugar to each serving. For her and Mr. Darcy, she filled the pewter containers.

The twins blew on the top before carefully taking a sip.

"Oh, Miss Elizabeth, it's the best," Jake proclaimed.

"I like the teapot." Rebekah traced the flowers on the handle with her fingers. "I like pink."

They enjoyed their beverages so much that the two adults forgot the potatoes frying in the pan.

"Something's burning," Jake exclaimed.

Hurrying to the fireplace, Elizabeth grabbed a spoon to stir the vegetables so they could get less dark brown on the other side. Only a small portion had scalded black. Deciding she would eat that section of their meal, she chose to pay more attention to what was cooking.

Peering into the pot, she saw the apple chunks bobbing in the boiling water. There was no fear of them burning or sticking to the pot. At least, she hoped.

"It is my job to set the dishes on the table," Rebekah stated.

"It is my job to keep the water bucket full," offered Jake.

Elizabeth praised them for being responsible. "Then my task will be to ensure the potatoes do not burn any more than they already have."

Mr. Darcy said, "There is a large woodpile under the eaves. I will bring in more wood." He looked toward Jake. "Since the water buckets are already filled, would you be willing to assist me?"

"Boy, would I," he declared, rushing over to take Darcy by the hand.

Finally relaxing, Elizabeth's mind dulled. Battered and bruised by wood and rocks, plus the frigid cold, she felt weak. Intense fear had a fierce hold on Elizabeth for the minutes they were in the water, exhausting her. And they had taken refuge in a cottage with no chaperones or servants. Once they were warm inside and out, they would make their way back to Longbourn. Then, they would deal with whatever consequences were in store.

* * *

Their meal was good only because they were famished. What potatoes and cabbage were not burned were not quite cooked through. Darcy had never been fastidious about what he was served (except for kale, of course), so the crispy edges of the potatoes with their soft centers were delicious on his tongue. The water in the large pot had boiled down, leaving an apple mush behind that was a sweet complement to the savory. With their stomachs full, the children's heads began to nod over their bowls, signaling that it was time to put them to bed.

Rebekah slid off her chair to stand at his side. Without a word, she put her bony knee on his thigh and her arm around his neck. Settling on Darcy's lap, she leaned her full weight against him, sighing once she was finally comfortable.

Her eyes captured his attention.

"What may I do for you, Miss Rebekah?" he asked.

She giggled. "I'm just plain Bekah, sir." Tucking her head into the curve of his neck, she added, "Did you used to be little, sir?"

He chuckled to himself. "I did. Why do you ask?"

"Because Mama said that her and Papa used to be little too. I will be big someday. When I am old, I will have a house with a black dog and a pink blanket on my bed." She pulled her head away from him. "Guess what color my curtains will be?"

"Pink?" Darcy said.

Rebekah grinned up at him, her palm under her chin. "No, I will have white curtains to let the sunshine in. I love the sunshine more than I love pink." She tapped her fingers on his cheek. "What color are your curtains in your house?"

Darcy had two houses, one on his estate of Pemberley and the other in London. He pondered how to respond. "Let us see, in the blue drawing room at my London house, I have blue curtains. The yellow sitting room has yellow curtains. The master's chambers with dark green wallpaper have… What do you think, Miss Rebekah?"

"What color are your rugs?"

"They are dark green, blue, scarlet red, brown, and gold." He struggled to recall the colors even though they had been in his chambers for the past five years.

"Gold. Your curtains would be gold," she replied. "But you could have brown like chocolate if you wanted."

Jake said, "Our Papa gave us chocolate one time."

Rebekah added, "We tried not to eat it too fast, but it was good. I like chocolate."

Elizabeth said, "I like chocolate too. Very much."

"Will you bring me chocolate sometime?" Rebekah asked, the twinkle in her eyes almost as bright as Elizabeth's.

Without hesitation, he promised that he would. The little urchin was burrowing into his heart, and he was doing little to stop her. She was not the only female in the cottage who affected him. Miss Elizabeth Bennet had already made inroads into his very being. If he were not careful, he would promise her far more than sweets from the candy shop.

Elizabeth smiled at Jake, who came to stand beside her. "Jake, please tell me what sort of work you hope to do when you grow up?"

The boy shrugged. "I wanted to be just like my papa, but now I don't know how. He kept books with lots of numbers in them. Sometimes those numbers made him frown, but mostly they made him and Mama happy."

"Numbers are amazing," Elizabeth agreed. "What of you, Rebekah? What dreams do you have of how you will fill your time when you are bigger?"

The little girl replied, "I want to paint and draw."

"Aw, Bekah, you'd just make all the flowers and animals pink," Jake said.

"I love pink," said Rebekah.

"I love pink too," Elizabeth agreed.

Jake asked Darcy, "What do you do now that you are big?"

"What do I do?" Darcy gave the boy's question consideration before answering. *How could he describe his multitude of responsibilities so a lad could understand?* "I have a large property with many acres of crops, herds, and flocks. The number of servants who care for my needs is large. It takes hours of oversight to keep everything running smoothly."

Jake nodded. "Do you have any children?"

"I have no wife," Darcy exclaimed at the unexpected query.

"Yeah, I don't either," Jake admitted before asking Elizabeth if there were more apples.

Darcy chuckled. Other than Georgiana, who never spoke unless prodded and who would never express an opinion for fear of being castigated, he was unused to the plain speaking of a child.

Little Rebekah was quiet. Nevertheless, she, like her brother, expressed her opinions freely. Was it because they had been brought up in a society with far less constraints? Or was it the parents themselves who encouraged their children to speak up?

Darcy could not keep himself from wondering if Georgiana was timid due to their father's discouraging opinions other than his own. *Good lord!* Had Darcy been so like their father that she still felt like she would be chastised if she spoke?

His stomach began to ache. The rake Georgiana almost eloped with presented himself as eloquent and pleasant. George Wickham could charm the pantaloons off…well, Darcy could easily picture him gently encouraging Georgiana to express herself to his rapt attention. No wonder his sister trusted Wickham! The rogue helped her see her value, something Darcy had never known he should do.

Blast! How had he not known the suffering his silence cost his sister? Why did he think following closely in his father's footsteps was the wisest path?

"Mr. Darcy, are you well?" Elizabeth turned toward him from where she had been sitting on the hearth. Her skin carried a lovely blush from the heat of the fire. Yet, it was her eyes that drew him in. For an instant, he wanted to lay his sins bare, hoping she would comfort him as she did the children. Would she?

* * *

Elizabeth tucked the quilt at the foot of the bed so the children would not pull the blanket off as they slept. Sitting on the edge, she reflected on how close they had come to losing Jake and Rebekah. Such precious little souls whose life had been arduous.

"Are you well, Miss Elizabeth?" Darcy whispered from across the room as he sorted through the remaining clothing.

She looked at the man, studying him closely. He had both hurt her vanity and pleased her. He was above his company and humble enough to wear someone else's old boots. With his finely tailored garments replaced by rugged togs and his hair curling in the warm, damp air, he was frightfully handsome. He was an amazing man!

"I am not quite certain how to reply, sir." She stood to join him at the armoire. "May I brew another pot of tea?"

The success of their earlier meal was more dependent on the hunger of the recipients. She was on much more solid ground, offering tea. Darcy kept the kettle on the stove filled with water and the fireplace with wood. Therefore, it was an easy task to measure out the leaves.

She saw the children sleeping before joining him at the table. "I will confess that my inclination and training tempt me to politely tell you that all is well with me. Then I would, equally as politely, ask about your welfare. However, circumstances have left me unnerved."

He nodded.

"Mr. Darcy, I will not lie to you since we are here due to the decisions of others. The children, in their inexperience, thinking running away was their only option, chose the potential for safety and hope over harm. Escaping Mr. Ralph Simms is understandable. My father chose to ignore his responsibilities to his family, our tenants, those affected by the collapse of the pond, and the land itself." She leaned closer. "Both you and I also made choices. For as much as I did not think before I leapt into the boat, your decision to rescue us rather than ride back to Netherfield Park for help was the saving of us all. Had it not been for you, sir, there would have been no way for me to hold onto the children and make our way to safety. We have all suffered injuries, but you, sir, have suffered the most. I cannot look at your shoulder without regret that the choices Jake, Rebekah, and myself made brought you harm."

Unabashedly, she let the tears gathered at the corner of her eyes streak down to her chin. "I fear that my taxed emotions and physical exhaustion will spur me to speak without restraint if I do not stop myself now."

He attempted to reassure her. "Now that you are warm, I shall return to Netherfield Park. From my estimation, we were in the water for ten to fifteen minutes. My guess is that we are approximately one and a half miles from the stone bridge where I first saw the three of you. There is enough sunlight remaining that I should find my way easily enough."

Rain pounded against the windows flanking the front door. His trek would be miserable.

"Elizabeth, I hesitate to leave you here. You will be caring for the children under primitive conditions. Additionally, our hosts may return before I do. They may resent discovering that we have encroached upon them." He ran his hands through his hair. Reaching across the table, he took her hand in his.

There had been contact between them from the second he entered the water, his strong arms wrapped around her and the children. In the skiff, pressed so closely as they were, it would have been a challenge for someone to determine where his body ended and hers began. She had seen his bare feet, the skin of his shoulder, and his forearms. Despite this, the gentle touch of his palm sent sparks shooting up her arm, threatening to singe the fabric of her...

Her eyes popped open.

"My clothing! What will my family think when they find my coat and bonnet next to the river? *Good heavens!* Would they assume...? I can hardly think of it. My father knew I was upset with him when I walked out of Longbourn. Did he think I was bereft of hope to the point that I ended it all?"

Elizabeth's stomach churned.

"And what of the others? Jane will mourn, her heart genuinely broken. Mary will piously condemn me for doing the unthinkable. Kitty and Lydia would fight over my lace fichu and the shoe roses I had purchased the last time I was in London. What of my mother? Will she be relieved at having one less daughter to marry off?"

Using her free hand, Elizabeth wiped away her tears. Her speech bubbled forth unrestrainedly.

"Unless Ralph Simms complains about the children being missing... No, he will likely miss his skiff more than Jake and

Rebekah. Unless he complains, there would be nothing to tie me to a boat."

Her imagination ran wild. She could see in her mind's eye her father and eldest sister pacing the length of the river, looking for her as her mother wailed loudly from the upper windows of the house.

Elizabeth was upset with her father, but that did not mean she no longer loved him.

"Elizabeth," Darcy whispered. "Think how relieved they will be when we unite you again."

Her heart was too full to speak. Shaking her head, Elizabeth closed her eyes tightly, her turbulent feelings overwhelming her. She had no more energy to worry or fret, no strength to consider the motives of her past or any options for her future. All she knew was that their stomachs were full; they were warm.

"Sir, I fully comprehend why you need to return to Netherfield Park. Yet, I worry for your safety. You are injured. You are equally exhausted. Once you step outside the cottage, you will be soaked again. There are not many hours left before the sun begins to set. The most direct path to Mr. Bingley is likely following the river, where the bank is softened from the deluge. The rain will hamper your visibility. As well, wearing boots that do not fit will slow you down, possibly endangering you further in the rocks and mud." She shuddered. "I know why you are going, yet I protest for your own safety that you are doing so."

He studied her face.

She knew she looked wretched. Her hairpins were gone. Her face was cut and likely bruised. The borrowed day dress was a horrid shade of greenish yellow. Elizabeth wished he would look away.

"I thank you for your concern." Mr. Darcy lowered his

eyes to the table before gazing upon her again. "As well, I appreciate your concern for your family's sensibilities. With the return of a saddled horse with no rider to the barn, I, too, am probably the source of Bingley's concern. Despite this, for the same reason as you, I have no regrets for attempting a rescue. Your life is precious to me, Elizabeth. The children are alive because of you. Had you not joined them, they would never have passed the first bend. I would have seen nothing but an empty boat bobbing upside down when I looked at the river. We, the both of us, made choices that changed their lives and ours. You are intelligent. You probably can guess what is to come. We will face the consequences together."

He stood. "I shall leave now. Pray, explain to the children why I am gone should they wake before I return."

Elizabeth selected a tattered coat from the drawer, holding it out to him. When he turned to face her after pushing his arms down the too-short sleeves, she automatically reached up to smooth the wool over his shoulders. Where she had done the same to her father many times, this feeling of intimacy was far different.

"Elizabeth," he whispered.

Her movement stilled. Her heart was overwhelmed. Her senses were on high alert until all she could see or think of was Darcy.

* * *

GAZING DOWN AT HER LOVELINESS, he knew the exact moment she became aware of the change in him. His Elizabeth was not a reticent gal. No, she peered up at him, her eyes even more beautiful than Rebekah's. Elizabeth Bennet set his soul on fire. He wanted to hold her, to pull her closer until her heart pounded against his own.

"Sir?" she whispered, the invitation still in the air when he lowered his mouth toward hers, her eyelids flickering closed.

She tasted of sunshine and hope.

In that infinitesimal moment in time, he felt as close to perfection as he ever would. With one final touch of his lips to hers, he said, "My leaving is not a parting, Elizabeth, it is a promise."

CHAPTER 15

Howling winds blew the rain sideways and assaulted him when he stepped outside the cottage, piercing through the layers of his borrowed garments. Hurrying to the river, Darcy found a trail leading back the way they came and toward Meryton.

Elizabeth was correct. The misfitting boots made walking a challenge. The toes pinched. His heels slid up and down with each step. He would need to watch his footing, which would slow his progress.

Elizabeth Bennet was everything lovely. More than that, she had shown herself to be incredibly courageous and kind. Without a doubt, he inherently knew that nothing could have separated her from those children once they were under her care.

Her words soothed the ache in his shoulder, hands, arms, and everywhere on his body where the debris from the river collided with him. He noted the dark purple bruises on her arms; she wore more at her temple and chin. There was a scratch across her cheek. Her right eye was red and swollen. She looked like she had lost an epic battle at Gentleman Jackson's. No, he was not the only one with injuries. Yet, she never once complained, even being cautious not to wince in front of the children so they would not worry over her. Never had he known a woman like her.

Before he left the cottage, she cared for the wounds on his shoulder with a gentleness he had not felt since his mother tended his scraped knees.

Did she comprehend what her choice to protect Jake and Rebekah would do to her reputation? If anyone discovered them…no, even if they were able to find their way back to Meryton with no one seeing them, the fact that two innocent children would speak of their rescue would destroy her future. Was that the reason for her tears?

If Darcy followed the desires his father had carefully outlined for him, despite his growing affection for her, he could do little to help Elizabeth. His path was destined to be with the upper ten thousand. He was to select a lady of impeccable breeding and manners who would bear the next generation of Darcys while managing his household with the skill of a magician. Any admiration he currently had for Elizabeth would be deemed as fanciful and fleeting. It could go nowhere.

However, he was no longer living under his father's authority. For the most part, he understood the wisdom his parents imparted to him. Nonetheless, there were matters where Darcy's own conscience bade him follow a different course. Was this one of them?

Perhaps Elizabeth's father had arrangements in place to recover his financial losses should his life end prematurely. What parent possessed of an entailed property would not? Except, Mr. Bennet had proven himself to be lazy and self-absorbed. Did he care for anyone other than himself? That he chose to manage Longbourn poorly was not a good reflection of his attitude toward acting responsibly toward others.

But his own daughters? Would he not extend himself for them? How would he treat his second daughter once she was safely at home? Would he welcome her and shield her from gossip, or would he shun her, forcing her to make her way alone?

If Darcy chose not to offer for her, perhaps he could supplement any funds that Longbourn could provide. Settling a few thousand on Miss Elizabeth would allow her a small cottage in a distant farm community where she could quietly make a good life if she chose. Except, he could never see the lady he was coming to know being content with merely existing.

What had he truly meant when he said his departure was a promise? The words were easy to utter. He was not the sort to ramble without thought. Was he telling Elizabeth that he would protect her by setting her up to be independent of her family? Or was he ultimately committed to offering her his hand in marriage?

His sigh was lost in the wind. His father often preached that the problems of others were not his problem. Yet, had that led to Gerald Darcy's happiness? Not at all.

As Darcy stepped over a pile of stones, he tried to see into the distance to measure his progress as he walked.

The salient question to be answered at that point was, why had he jumped? He had overcome more than a decade of fear of the water! He had gone exactly where he had been forbidden and was glad for it.

Was it because he felt the children's fear in his own heart? Yes, to a measure, which was true. Was it because there was no one else? Perhaps. But had someone else been there to help, would Darcy have extended himself? Or would he have been like his father and stepped back, waiting for someone more suitable to their station to jump in? Was it a need to be the hero to a lady he could admit to himself that he was growing to love? His father would never have accepted Elizabeth Bennet as the future mistress of Pemberley.

Again, he reflected on the fact that he was not Gerald Darcy.

Darcy wiped his free hand over his face, the scratches on his palm rough against his cheek. What sort of person was he? Who was he? Was he a mirror of his father? Of course, he admired Gerald Darcy. In many ways, Pemberley's prosperity was due to his father's tireless efforts. At the same time, his firm will and insistence on the highest standards made it hard for other mere mortals to live up to the senior Darcy's requirements. Foremost expected to measure up was the son and heir to Pemberley, Fitzwilliam Darcy.

Wiping the rain from his eyes, he considered his choices during the past five years since his father was gone. Had he been wrong to continue in the path of his sire? Had he made life hard for others by insisting on the same high standards? What of Georgiana? Was her inability to forgive herself a response to his harsh requirements? It was sobering to think upon.

What of Richard? His appeal before he left that Darcy learn to be happy was confusing. With the events of the day, Darcy thought he was beginning to understand.

He admired Elizabeth's kindness to others. He was drawn to kindness. Why, he wondered? Was it because it was lacking in him?

Something inside his chest stirred at the memory of Rebekah Simmons moving her face so her soft breath tickled his neck. What he held in his arms was precious. Jake and Rebekah Simmons were worth everything, as was Elizabeth Bennet. Life itself was precious. That he had a hand in saving them was an act of valor, something he had every right to be proud of.

Fire kindled inside him. His own act of kindness in

coming to their rescue stirred him to the depths of his heart. Pride in the rightness to jump in to help threatened to overwhelm him. It energized him. He felt a sense of purpose far above that of being known as a good steward of the land, a loyal older brother to Georgiana, or the master over many.

He had been trained since infancy to value position over everything. Yet, he now knew there was something more precious. To pursue a course of extending himself to others would set him against everything his father stood for. Could he do it? Would he do it? *Who is the real Fitzwilliam Darcy?*

The answer was simple. For as much as Darcy knew that his father would insist that she was not for him, he could no longer deny his feelings. He wanted that kiss. Dreams were made from a response like hers. He craved her touch. He felt a passion he had not experienced before. He needed her for him to be complete.

He was a man in love with the best woman in the world. He would do all within his power to make Elizabeth Bennet his wife.

Contentment with the decision filled him, bringing him peace. As Richard suggested, Darcy would pursue happiness with his full might.

Grinning despite the inclement weather, he held onto a fencepost to navigate around another pile of stones. Darcy's heart started pounding. He was perilously close to the river. His fingers slipped on the fencepost at the same time the boots slid in the mud. His head smashed onto a rock buried under the water. Within a heartbeat, he no longer felt the cold.

* * *

J. DAWN KING

ELIZABETH STOOD AT THE WINDOW, watching his progress until she could see him no more. She worried about his safety. No, she did more than worry.

When he bent to brush a kiss on the temple of each child, yearning shot through her, almost knocking her off her feet. In that moment, she could no longer lie to herself that her affections were unattached. She had done the unthinkable by falling head over heels in love with Mr. Fitzwilliam Darcy.

***

AN HOUR LATER, the children woke hungry enough to eat more potatoes.

"Where is he?" Rebekah demanded.

"Mr. Darcy has gone for help."

When Elizabeth walked the three miles from Longbourn to Netherfield Park, it had taken an hour. The pathway was well-traveled, making it less strenuous to navigate than the narrow walkway Darcy would follow. Still, he must have made progress toward reaching Mr. Bingley's residence.

Adding more wood to the fire, she wished for a slice of bread, not realizing she had stated her wishes aloud.

"I love bread," said Rebekah.

Jake said, "Mama made bread every day. She poked it and smacked it on the table until flour rose into the air. Then she put it in a cupboard to dry, or something. It grew and grew and grew until she stuck it into the oven." He rubbed his belly. "She used to give Papa both ends dripping with butter and jam. After he was gone, she gave each of us the end... except we didn't have any more jam."

Rebekah added, "Mama put love in her bread because she told us so."

Jake nodded.

Their simple comments about their lives before they

arrived in England humbled Elizabeth, reminding her that in comparison to what the children had weathered, she suffered little.

"Do you have a Papa and Mama still?" Jake asked.

"I do. We live in a large house we call Longbourn. I have four sisters. Jane is older by almost two years. Mary arrived after me, as did Kitty and Lydia."

"What does your papa do?"

Jake's innocent question stirred her.

"Like Mr. Darcy, he manages a large property."

Satisfied with her reply, the children chased each other around the room.

Elizabeth pondered the lad's innocent query. The simple truth was that no matter how active her imagination was, she could not picture Thomas Bennet as an active participant in oversight of the land. She could only see him insisting on remaining behind because he had the important task of reading for his pleasure to attend. Even had he known the danger to the children, he would have felt bad for them as he waited for someone else to rescue them. Then he would have become absorbed in his latest book, completely forgetting about the plight of the twins until the report of their survival or demise came to his ears. Then, and only then, would he express sorrow or joy before returning to where he had marked the page so he could begin again.

When was the last time she could remember her father participating in their lives? Was it when each daughter entered society? No, he had not attended either Kitty or Lydia's come out at the assembly. He was there for hers, was he not? No, her uncle Phillips had stood up with her for her first set. What of Jane? Elizabeth's mind shot further into the past.

A memory of her mother heavy with child struck Elizabeth. Jane was about ten years old since she had prominent front teeth. The day was sunny and warm. Her mother had requested the pony cart to take them to the river for a picnic. Cook had already packed a lovely luncheon with strawberries in one of the bowls. Elizabeth loved strawberries.

Anxious to get started, Elizabeth repeatedly asked when they could leave. Each time, her mother would reply, "We are waiting for your father."

After several hours had crept by, her mother instructed their housekeeper to place the food on one of the small tables in the drawing room. Stubbornly, she insisted that the lowliest groom in the stables be invited inside to partake. To the shock of Longbourn's servants, Mrs. Francine Bennet served the groom like he was their equal. The mistress of the house refused to eat. By the time her father left his study, the opportunity for a lovely picnic by the water was gone, as was all the food.

Elizabeth and Jane were in their shared bedchamber that night when they heard the loud voices of their parents yelling at each other.

Jane vowed, "I will never scream at my husband."

Full young, Elizabeth recalled replying, "I will never give my husband reason to yell at me."

She wondered if she could keep that promise. The thought brought her to tears, and Elizabeth hated crying. Even worse, she hated that her changed circumstances moved her to weep.

Discovering that her father placed his family in a precarious financial position was crushing. Of course, she had long known that the Bennet daughters were not well provided for since neither parent had done anything to increase their portions. Knowing beyond doubt that being in close company with Darcy and the twins would destroy whatever hope she had for a happy future unless he offered for her added to her grief. Yet, she was not made to mourn.

Rubbing her cheeks dry with the hem of her borrowed day dress, Elizabeth sat up straight. She was alive. She had a measure of intelligence. And she had two children who needed help more than she did.

Mr. Darcy was a cautious man. Yes, he had made a promise, but he never implied or directly stated that he meant marriage. In fact, other than a kiss, he had given her no reason to hope for an offer from him. His rank was high enough above hers to provide her with no basis for dreaming they might have a future together.

Her heart felt like it was bleeding inside for, after their kiss and his words of promise, there was nothing she wanted more than to become his bride.

CHAPTER 16

For the millionth time, Elizabeth peered out the window, only to see no activity, no approaching savior—only the wind buffeting the cottage as the rain continued to pound against the glass.

Enough time passed that Darcy must have arrived at Netherfield Park. She prayed he was not harmed. He was a man of integrity. She was confident that his devotion to the children would have him return as soon as humanly possible. And what of his promise to her? Without a doubt, Elizabeth knew he would keep his word.

She gasped, her hands covering her mouth. He kissed her. A true gentleman would never act in such a manner unless his honor was engaged. Fitzwilliam Darcy was a gentleman.

He will return. He will offer for me. We will have a happy future.

If only he would return. Was he injured? Was he, at that moment, lying in the mud somewhere, slowly freezing to death?

Worry plagued her.

Suddenly, Rebekah stopped her play.

"I hear someone."

Rushing to the door, Elizabeth flung it open to welcome the man who owned her heart. Except, it was not Darcy. Instead, two strangers were making their way up the walkway.

* * *

Mr. and Mrs. Whitmer were a lovely couple who were away for the day to spend time with their daughter. Although they were surprised to discover unexpected guests, they quickly welcomed Elizabeth and the children to their humble home.

After explaining how they came to be at the cottage, Elizabeth asked, "By chance, do you know how far we are from Netherfield Park? The gentleman who saw to our safety left hours ago for help."

Mr. Whitmer said, "The big house is almost a mile away as the crow flies, longer by pony cart. Is this where you are from?"

Elizabeth replied, "Longbourn. And the children recently arrived from America." She smoothed the skirt she was wearing. "Mr. Darcy's destination was Netherfield Park. He was staying with friends."

"Word from my neighbors was that a dam partially let loose upriver so your account rings true. Since the river did not overflow and damage our immediate area, the majority of the structure must continue to stand."

"Mr. Darcy observed the same, sir." Elizabeth was exceedingly grateful the damage from her father's negligence appeared to be to them alone.

Mrs. Whitmer offered biscuits from a tin stuffed behind a narrow shelf of books. "Mr. Whitmer will eat them all if I do not hide them."

Jake said, "I would eat all of them too. These are wonderfully good."

Elizabeth agreed.

Mrs. Whitmer asked, "Did your mum bake the same sort of biscuits in America, Jacob?"

The lad chuckled before saying, "Just call me Jake, please. Mama and Papa only called me Jacob when I was in trouble for something."

"Trouble? You?" Mrs. Whitmer teased before handing him another biscuit. "I can already tell that you are a sweet boy. Miss Rebekah, you are a precious dear."

"I'm Bekah." The little girl leaned against Elizabeth. "When will Mr. Darcy come back?"

Glancing at the darkness outside the window, Elizabeth guessed, "I suppose we shall see him in the morning."

Mr. and Mrs. Whitmer stood. "We shall offer you our bed for the night."

Elizabeth deeply appreciated their kindness. "We thank you. If you approve, I believe the three of us would much rather curl up on a blanket in front of the fire. After being so thoroughly cold, it appeals to us greatly."

"Very well." Mrs. Whitmer pulled several quilts from a cupboard behind the bed. "Please do not be disturbed when my husband gets up during the night to tend the fire. We, too, like it warm."

Minutes later, Elizabeth stretched out on the floor, resting her head on her arm. Gazing into the flames, she desperately wondered about the whereabouts of Mr. Darcy. Was he safe? Was he well? Was he warm?

When dawn began to make its appearance known, she had not moved nor slept. She refused to rest until she knew what had happened to Darcy.

* * *

His body shook. His teeth chattered. His skin was on fire. His throat was raw. His mouth was dry. His eyes felt like they were filled with sand. The groans coming from him sounded distant. Never had Darcy been as miserable.

"Elizabeth!" he shouted, though it sounded like he had whispered.

"Hush now, young man. Save your energy for healing. Have a cool drink. Do you need help?"

He did not recognize the voice. When the man helped him to sit up, Darcy noted his surroundings.

He was in a building like the cottage where he left Elizabeth and the children.

"Where am I?" he asked.

The man chuckled. "Elsinore Castle."

"Shakespeare," Darcy whispered. "Hamlet."

"Yes, you have found me out."

The man helped Darcy lay back before he stepped into the light. He bowed before saying, "I am Mr. Alfred Pierce, an educator whose love for too many bottles of fine wine left me impoverished and unemployable. Fortunately, a colleague did not need this small portion of his property at Waterston Cove, a small village near the river Lea. He is not in residence. The cottage is impossible to see unless you arrive by boat. For my health and entertainment, I occasionally wander the river to see if anything of interest washes up on the bank. To my surprise, two days ago, you made an appearance."

"Two days?" Darcy was horrified. Elizabeth and the children needed help. He tried to sit up on his own. Weakness rendered him unable to get out of bed. Determination had him hanging onto the bedpost. "Elizabeth!"

"Yes. You have said her name often. Is she your wife?"

Ignoring the query, Darcy attempted to stand on his own. The effort nearly dropped him to his knees. His speech was uneven. He had to stop after each word. "Elizabeth and two children were in the boat. I tried to save them. Capsized."

The man's face paled. "I saw no boat nor any others. I am terribly sorry. I hope they made it to safety."

Darcy sat on the bedside, his face resting in his palms. Despite the agony in his throat, his voice was firm. "I left them in a stranger's cottage to await my return. I was walking to Netherfield Park to get help when I slipped and fell into the water. I promised to rescue them. I need to rescue them. Please, help me."

Mr. Pierce hesitated. "Netherfield Park. Those three must be close to the river between here and there, am I correct?"

Darcy nodded. "I must help them now." Jumping to his feet, Darcy quickly discovered his intentions were far more than his body could manage. Within seconds, he collapsed back on the bed, and his whole world blackened.

***

When the children woke without Darcy's being there, the twins' playfulness vanished. Like Elizabeth, they were deeply concerned.

"Did he die like Papa and Mama?" Rebekah asked, piercing Elizabeth's heart.

"No!" Elizabeth insisted. "I do not know what has happened, but I refuse to believe that anything is wrong. Something necessary has delayed him. That is all."

"Will we wait for him here?" Jake wondered.

"Allow me to find out." She asked Mr. Whitmer for his suggestion.

With the rain having stopped, he informed them that he had a pony cart where they could take a narrow road, winding around the hillsides to reach Longbourn. The journey should take the morning.

Once their stomachs were full and they were comfortably bundled in Mrs. Whitmer's blankets, they were off.

For the length of the journey, neither child made a sound. That suited Elizabeth. If only Darcy had known about the road. Weeping inside as she showed her bravest face from without, Elizabeth kept her eyes fixed toward Meryton.

***

Jane ran into Elizabeth's embrace. "You are returned! We were frantic, Lizzy. One of the newly arrived militia officers discovered your coat and bonnet by the river. I was afraid… afraid…oh, Lizzy. You are come back to us."

"Lizzy!" Her father rushed to her. "I feared we lost you." Wrapping his arms around both of his daughters, he pulled them close. "Thank god you are home."

The warmth of their embrace was a comfort. The children, who had their arms tightly around her middle, were getting squished.

"Papa, Jane, I would like to introduce you to Mr. Whitmer. He and his wife offered us shelter. These two brilliant children are Jacob and Rebekah Simmons. They have recently been guests of Mr. Ralph Simms."

Papa's brow arched before he bowed deeply to the man. "I am in your debt." With a brush of his fingers on Elizabeth's cheeks, he said, "Welcome to Longbourn. Yes, even you two young ones are welcome. Come, Mr. Whitmer, to my study. I need to repay you for your goodness and sacrifice."

"That be mighty kind of you, Mr. Bennet. However, I did not return these three to Longbourn for that purpose. If you do not mind, Mrs. Whitmer will worry if it gets dark and I am not there."

Elizabeth curtsied. "Please allow us to send something from Longbourn's kitchen, sir. While they wrap the food items, I want to collect something from my chambers for Mrs. Whitmer." Asking the twins to remain with Jane, Elizabeth hurried up the stairs. In the place where she stored her few treasured items, she found her blue and cream paisley shawl purchased by her aunt from Paris. The particular shade of blue was lovely.

With sincere gratitude, Elizabeth again thanked the man and his wife for the hospitality they showed. "I will never forget you," Elizabeth promised.

Jane knelt to the same level as the twins. "If you would come with me, we shall sit by the warm fire. There I will read you some of my sister's favorite stories. They are filled with adventure and wild animals. Will you come?"

"Will I!" Jake blurted.

Even though Rebekah hesitated, where her brother went, she followed.

Elizabeth directed her full attention to her father. "Papa, might I speak with you privately?"

Before the door to his study closed, she insisted, "We must send for Mr. Bingley immediately. Papa, Mr. Darcy is missing after rescuing us from the water. A search party must be gathered and sent on their way."

"Mr. Darcy!" Her father was incredulous. "Where has he gone? Why are you involved?"

Keeping the tale as short as possible, Elizabeth explained the events of the day prior. Within moments, Mr. Bennet penned a note while Elizabeth ran to the stable to have their lone horse readied. By the time the groom was at the front portico, Mr. Bennet handed him the note with instructions to ride as quickly as the horse was able to Netherfield Park.

In less than thirty minutes, Mr. Bingley and Mr. Hurst were at Longbourn.

* * *

A NOISE STARTLED DARCY AWAKE.

In his dreams, he finally made his way to Longbourn in time to see Mr. Bennet hand Elizabeth off to a strange man at the Meryton chapel. His host, Mr. Pierce, shouted congratulations to Mr. Ralph Simms and his new bride.

Mrs. Bennet beamed at having one of her daughters wed, while Mr. Bennet praised Mr. Simms for marrying a compromised woman who dared to spend hours alone with Mr. Darcy.

"No!" Darcy wanted to scream. *We were not alone! She is not ruined! She is priceless. She is worthy! And she is mine!*

Sitting up, he rubbed his eyes, his heart pounding. The narrow room at the back of the cottage where he slept was pitch dark. Because there were no windows, he had no idea if it was day or night.

Throwing the bedclothes aside, he again attempted to get out of bed. This time, he was able to stand on his own. Tentatively, he took a step. Then, he took another. It was too much. He was determined to do everything necessary to find Elizabeth. He must get strong enough to leave Mr. Pierce's abode. There was something mysterious surrounding his host. Darcy had no desire to be caught up in whatever activities had him hiding from society.

Laying back on the bed, he counted to three hundred. Cautiously, he stood for a second before trying another step. His knees shook. His hands quivered. Beads of sweat dotted his brow. His chest felt like an elephant rested on his breastbone. When he coughed, it shook his whole body. He needed to lay back down.

In spite of his weakness, Darcy's mind was active. He had already asked Mr. Pierce to send correspondence to Bingley or Richard. However, his host had no supplies to pen a letter. Nor could he afford postage. The few coins he received from his benefactor were spent solely on food. In this way, there was no ability to purchase wine. Additionally, his host refused to leave the property out of fear he might succumb to temptation.

His excuses seemed paltry. The lack of books and paper belied his claim as an educator.

Darcy was on his own. The only way to find Elizabeth and return her to her home was to gain the strength to walk out the door under his own power.

Counting again to three hundred, Darcy tried again, pleased when he could stand longer than he did before.

Elizabeth. Be safe. Be strong. I love you.

CHAPTER 17

When Mr. Charles Bingley was in Darcy's presence, he did not appear to be the sort of man in charge. Nevertheless, now that there was a threat to his friend, the younger man took command. His eyes were shot through with red, his hair was disheveled, and his clothing looked like it had been slept in. Mr. Hurst looked the same.

Elizabeth was grateful.

"Miss Elizabeth, I am both appalled and comforted that you were with Darcy. Appalled that you faced life-threatening danger but comforted that he was not alone. For this, I sincerely offer my appreciation." Mr. Bingley bowed. "We had not seen nor heard from Darcy since he departed Netherfield yesterday. We knew to worry when his horse returned without him. Hurst, myself, and my servants searched the property and beyond until darkness fell. We only stopped then because the rain extinguished the torches. When his clothing was found on the bridge, we feared the worst. Since daybreak, we have been concentrating our search along the river.

"I sent an express to his cousin, Colonel Fitzwilliam, last evening. I hated to write to him of my suspicions, but there is Darcy's sister to inform and protect. I shall contact him with this new information immediately. If he remains in England, he will be here soon. I will also approach Colonel Forster of the militia. He can bring his troops to the other side of the stone bridge to search a larger area on each side of the river." To her father, he said, "If you would remain here, we can use Longbourn as our base, reporting our efforts, so we do not duplicate coverage. We must find Darcy as soon as possible. Every minute he spends exposed to the elements increases his danger. I will find Colonel Forster now."

The gentlemen from Netherfield spun on their heels and left Longbourn. Not twenty minutes later, Colonel Forster, three of his men, and Mr. Bingley returned. Elizabeth could hear the chatter and swoons from her mother and younger sisters from the drawing room for having officers at Longbourn. Their flirting irritated her:

"Welcome to Longbourn, Colonel. My, do not your officers appear to the best advantage in their uniforms?"

"Well, good day! I am Miss Lydia Bennet, my mother's favorite. Lieutenant, what did you say your name was?"

In her mind, Elizabeth could see her youngest, most foolish sister approach the men with not one person stepping in to stop her.

"Mr. Wickham."

"Oh, yes, Mr. Wickham. Would we not stun the crowds at every ball with your fair looks and my raven hair? Why, I believe we are a match made in heaven." Lydia purred.

"Me too!" Kitty screeched. "I would look good paired with an officer too."

Jane attempted to bring a modicum of respectability with her soft censure, but it was to no avail.

"Papa!" Elizabeth pleaded with him to intercede.

He ignored her.

It was Mr. Bingley who ushered the officers to her father's room.

Elizabeth firmly closed the door behind them.

Mr. Bingley reported, "Hurst has taken a dozen militiamen to ride along the far side of the river. We are now able to extend the search."

Colonel Forster faced Elizabeth and ordered, "Tell us as much information as you remember about where you last saw Mr. Darcy."

Elizabeth did not hesitate. She described as much as she recalled, including the approximate length of time they were in the boat. She told him how to locate the Whitmer cottage.

The men, including Mr. Bingley, left immediately.

Elizabeth began pacing her father's study, appreciating that many of the stacks of books were gone.

To keep from imagining the worst about Darcy, she said, "I am proud of you, Papa. You followed through on your promise."

"Yes, well," he hesitated. "It is far too little too late, I am afraid. Nonetheless, these funds will be secreted away for Mrs. Bennet and your sisters to use in case I am sent to Marshalsea. I have located another man who is interested in the rest."

"What of the map?" she hesitated to ask. "It still resides in its place of dishonor. Will you not part with it too?"

"The map of Peru?" He pulled an aged leather tube from the top shelf, then tapped it against his palm. "I am keeping it as a reminder that not everyone who claims to be honest is honest, and not everything that looks valuable on the outside has any worth."

"Very good, Papa." Relief relaxed Elizabeth somewhat.

"Now, tell me, Daughter. You wear your anxiety openly for a man you once despised. You do love him, then?"

The simple question hit her like an arrow piercing her heart. How should she answer? Her feelings were new, something she wanted to hold and protect. To expose them to a man who lived to tease and ridicule, even though she loved her father, was unwise.

Elizabeth cautiously replied. "Papa, I fear for Mr. Darcy. He has no love of water, yet his path would have led him close to the river. He is a stranger to our portion of Hertfordshire. He could be lost, wandering the pathways in search of rescue. I do not know enough of him to know if he has a good sense of direction. Is he like me, where my internal compass always finds my way home? Or is he like Mary, who would never be able to get from here to Meryton and back without a sister to guide her? I do not know."

She was rambling. Nevertheless, it kept her mind occupied, far away from her true concern. In the darkest part of her mind, it was as if someone sketched an image of Darcy slipping on a wet rock, falling into the raging river, unable to call for help. Unable to breathe.

She pressed her hands to her chest. No, she refused to allow a waft of doubt inside where it would take on a life of its own. He was alive. He was well. He promised.

While the men searched, Elizabeth spent equal time with Jake and Rebekah. The lad wanted to play. The little girl needed stories to distract her. For Elizabeth, they were a link to the man who had her heart on edge. In comforting them, she consoled herself.

Every minute that passed felt like an hour. When the sun began to set with no word from the men, Elizabeth paced from one end of the drawing room to the other. The children followed silently behind her. Her family left them alone.

The mantel clock struck four times when they heard a loud pounding on the front door. Elizabeth's heart leapt into her throat. Barely keeping herself from rushing to the entrance hall, she held the hand of each child. Her family ran into the room.

It was him. It had to be him.

Except it was not. Mr. Bingley and Mr. Hurst followed a stranger inside.

"You are Miss Elizabeth?"

"I am."

"Colonel Richard Fitzwilliam at your service." He bowed.

The colonel was approximately Darcy's age, or maybe slightly older. He was only a few inches shorter, but his shoulders and arms were massive. His skin was weathered, and his eyes intelligent. Mud spattered his great coat and boots.

From his appearance and movements, he looked prepared for battle. *This is a man I can trust.*

"You did not find him?" Elizabeth asked, desperate for news.

The colonel replied, "Not as yet. We spoke with Mr. and Mrs. Whitmer. Mr. Whitmer was needed to help a neighbor repair damage from the wind, so he did not follow Darcy's footsteps after he returned home. When we arrived, the rain filled and hid my cousin's tracks. However, since we knew his direction, we canvased the whole area between there and here. Once the rain stops, I will lead the men back with torches to search further afield. Darcy is strong and determined. We will find him, I promise."

Jake asked, "Did you ride Excalibur?"

"I did." The colonel looked surprised at the question.

"Then you will find him," the lad insisted.

"I thank you for your confidence, young man." To Elizabeth's father, he said, "We will not stop again until we have news, so do not expect us." He bowed. "Ladies." The colonel stepped closer to Elizabeth. "We will not stop until we find him."

"Please, do." Elizabeth lifted her chin. She had every reason to hope.

* * *

As the hours passed, Darcy's cough deepened, seizing him harshly. His dreams were filled with Elizabeth. Always, she was just out of reach.

After one such nightmare, he woke to fresh air entering through the open door. Summoning what was left of his reserves of strength, he crawled from the bed to discover the main door swinging back and forth in the breeze.

The air cooled his skin. Before he took two steps into the room, Mr. Pierce entered, a load of wood in his arms.

Dropping his burden on the small hearth, he said, "Do take a seat before you fall, young man. I fear I could not lift you if you fell on the floor. I shall make tea."

Darcy dropped into an overstuffed chair. For the first time, he was able to see his situation. Scratching his scruffy chin, he tipped his head back to ease the air into his lungs. When his breathing eased, he questioned his host.

"How long have I been here?"

"Two nights and three days." Mr. Pierce stoked the fire. "For most of the time, you have been incoherent. I feared for your survival, young man." He again stirred the coals before turning to sit on the hearth. "What is your name?"

"Darcy. Fitzwilliam Darcy."

"How did you come to be in the river?"

"I recall my feet slipping. I must have fallen."

"That explains the bloody gash at the back of your skull. Does your head still hurt?"

"It does, although far less than before."

"Hmm. Do you remember why you were on the river? I shall not tell you what you mumbled the first day you woke."

"Yes. A lady and two children needed rescue. I helped them to a cottage. Once they were warm, I left for help. I woke here."

"Elizabeth?"

Darcy did not know this man enough to share details of a woman precious to him. He nodded, renewing the pounding at the base of his skull.

"Mr. Pierce, I recall you telling me you would not be easily found. If others are searching for me, is there a way I can let them know of my location?"

His host cleared his throat. "Ah, yes. I understand your desire to be reunited with your loved ones. However, I cannot take a chance that word of where I am will find its way back to the wrong people."

"Your name is not Pierce?"

"It is not."

"Am I correct in believing that your being here has very little to do with abstinence from wine?."

"You are." Mr. Pierce, or whatever was his name, added, "Despite being dressed in simple clothing, from your speech, I can tell that you are an educated man. Oxford?"

"I am a Cambridge man."

"I see."

"Do you?" Darcy asked for he was frustrated at the man's reticence. Gulping in air and ignoring his sore throat, he stated, "I am the master of Pemberley in Derbyshire and Darcy House in London. My uncle is Hugh Fitzwilliam, Lord Matlock and—"

The man gasped as the color drained from his face. "Hugh Fitzwilliam? No!"

Sickening dread crept up Darcy's spine. He had no illusions where his uncle was concerned. "He deceived you? You are hiding from him?"

His host buried his face in his hands. "He ruined me.

When I sought justice, I foolishly assumed that others who had been taken in would gladly come forward to get their revenge. I stood alone. I escaped with help from someone whose older brother was trapped by Lord Matlock. My sole obligation is to remain out of sight and never mention that fraudulent transaction again. I owe my life to my benefactor. Your uncle would have us both killed without blinking his eyes if he knew where I was and my savior's involvement."

Bitter bile rose to the back of Darcy's throat. He loathed the actions of his uncle. That he used his iron fist to smite others with seeming impunity was a blight on the Fitzwilliam name.

"Allow me to reassure you. I am not my uncle, nor will I ever be."

Mr. Pierce rubbed his hands roughly on his cheeks, then said, "I have risked much by allowing you to remain here, Mr. Darcy. Under normal circumstances, I would welcome you. But I ask you to rest so you may gain your strength. You need to be with your Elizabeth. I need you to be gone."

In full agreement, Darcy made his way back to his bed. His body was weak, but his will was strong. Closing his eyes, he pictured Elizabeth holding the children in the water, protecting their lives as the little ones clung to her. He thought of her laughing when she realized she had burned the potatoes. But it was her kiss and the tender way she wrapped her arms around him that drove him back to his feet.

Mr. Pierce was correct. He needed to leave. He needed Elizabeth.

CHAPTER 18

When Colonel Fitzwilliam and Mr. Bingley arrived at Longbourn the day after Elizabeth returned home, their bloodshot eyes, unshaven whiskers, and soiled clothing spoke of their exhaustion more than words.

Kitty and Lydia had taken the children under their wings, keeping them in the nursery as distracted and entertained as possible.

Elizabeth was past the point of being able to pretend that all was well. Her self-assigned duty was to pace the drawing room until Darcy was found.

When there were no joyous exclamations of success from the men, no smiles of jubilation, she gritted her teeth. She could not, nor would she believe anything ill happened to Darcy.

Colonel Fitzwilliam cleared his throat. "We have covered every inch of Hertfordshire soil from here to the river Lea with no one seeing a sign of my cousin. Our next step is to travel throughout the villages on each side of the river. We will stop at every home, every barn, every hovel until we find Darcy."

"Thank you, Colonel. The dam?"

"You and the others were fortunate, Miss Elizabeth. There are two large logs wedged against the stone bridge amidst a tangle of debris. The rest of the dam appears intact. We have seen little destruction."

Relief flooded her. "Does your family know Mr. Darcy is missing?" she inquired.

"I hope not, or they will rush to Meryton, bringing confusion and distraction in their wake." The colonel's gaze moved to the window. "Should Father pressure the general for information about my whereabouts, he would learn of my reason for being here. Let us both pray that does not happen."

"Certainly, sir."

"We shall find him."

"I pray that you do."

As soon as the door closed behind the men, she stood vigil at the window again. *Where are you, Fitzwilliam Darcy? Come back to me.*

* * *

Mr. Pierce shared another serving of bone broth and a piece of dry toast. The crumbs played havoc with Darcy's scratchy throat, but he ate it anyway. Once the man left the room, Darcy swung his legs from the bed and stood. This time, his knees did not shake, and the muscles in his calves failed to quiver. Whether it was sheer determination or he was that much stronger mattered not to him. Fear at what Elizabeth suffered from his disappearance drove him to step toward a stand containing toiletries at the foot of his bed.

After a quick wash of his face and teeth, he pushed his feet into the borrowed boots, accepted the gift of a coat from the mysterious Mr. Pierce, and departed.

Once outside, he surveyed the landscape. Mr. Pierce was correct. Unless someone knew the exact location of his small abode, they would never see it. Looking back, Darcy could see nothing except a hillock surrounded by tall evergreen trees. There were no doors or windows visible. Even the smoke from the chimney streamed downriver with the wind.

Moving well away from the river, he set off toward Elizabeth. Mr. Pierce indicated that he was slightly more than four miles to Meryton, which would be two miles to Netherfield Park. If Elizabeth could cover that distance caring for her sister, then he would do it, even if he had to crawl to see his Elizabeth.

His knees shook. Each step seemed a monumental effort. His breathing was shallow. His chest felt like it was on fire. Ignoring his misery, Darcy pressed on.

* * *

OVER THE HOURS, Elizabeth reviewed her interactions with Darcy. With every recollection, her confidence in his promise grew. When Jane brought the children into the room, Elizabeth welcomed them with an embrace.

"Isn't he here yet?" Rebekah hurried to the window to look outside.

"Not yet." Elizabeth moved to join her.

"But it's raining. He'll be wet and cold."

"Yes, he will. However, do recall that he was wet and cold when he exited the river. He was strong enough to build a fire and bring in water."

Jake added, "Yeah, and he was strong enough to gather all the apples, which were much better than the potatoes."

"They were surprisingly good," Elizabeth agreed. An idea came to her. "Mr. Bingley, Mr. Hurst, and Colonel Fitzwilliam are searching for Mr. Darcy as we speak. I suggest we see how successful we can be at finding something that is hidden. If the three of us close our eyes tightly, Jane, who is the best at putting items where no one can find them, will hide something for us. Would you like to play?"

"Yes!" The twins jumped up and down.

"Very good. Now, let us close our eyes while Jane completes her task."

Immediately, their eyes closed. "Cover your ears so we do not hear pillows move or count her footsteps."

The children obeyed. Elizabeth did the same until she felt her sister's fingers on her arm.

"We are ready." She tapped the twins on the shoulder, their eyes popping open.

Jane said, "I have hidden a yellow button somewhere in the room. It is within reach of all three of you, so you do not need to climb on the furniture or move the chairs to find it. You may begin now."

The first place the twins searched was behind the pillows on the sofa. Next, they peered underneath the furniture. Their squeals of delight brought Elizabeth's other sisters to the room.

"Can we play too?" Lydia asked.

Kitty said, "Jane always finds the hardest places to hide."

"Sure," Jake replied before Elizabeth could answer.

With all of them searching, the game did not last long. The button was finally found by Rebekah when Kitty accidentally bumped a small table, jarring a piece of lace to the side. She held the button like it was a diamond.

"I found it."

Elizabeth and Jane praised her success.

Jake grumbled, "If only we could get back our tin box with the important papers inside. Then we'd have a future like Mama said."

In all her concern for Darcy, she forgot about the tin.

Deciding that performing an essential task of her own would help the time pass more quickly, Elizabeth said, "I believe it is time to pay Mr. Simms a call."

"Eww!" Kitty exclaimed as she and Lydia plugged their noses. "He never bathes. We must cross the street when he is near."

Jane said, "Perhaps you two would not mind continuing to play with the children while Lizzy and I ask Papa to accompany us to Mr. Simms's house."

The girls quickly agreed, then argued over who would be next to hide the button.

Elizabeth reminded them that the house rules were that whoever found the button was the next to hide it before leaving the room with Jane.

Her father readily consented. "Ralph Simms? I would never want my daughters to approach him alone. Of course, I will go."

Jake and Rebekah's laughter, coupled with her father's ready agreement, lightened her heart. With the hope of the colonel finding success, too, being in Darcy's presence would make that day her best.

By the time the stable had their old carriage ready, Jake and Lydia had each found the button. Lydia was the second best in the family at hiding, so the next round should take longer. When Elizabeth and the others left Longbourn, the children failed to notice being so well entertained with the game.

* * *

Although Elizabeth was determined to give Mr. Simms a piece of her mind, her father used the head of his walking stick to rap on the door.

Ralph Simms was the antithesis of a gentleman. His hair

stood on end, his shirt buttons were undone, and the fingernails scratching his chin were rimmed in filth. To think that Jake and Rebekah lived with that man was sickening.

"Pardon me, Mr. Simms. My daughter came across two young children who claim you as uncle."

Mr. Simms interrupted. "Them brats stole my boat. If I see them again, I'll turn them in. They'll hang for what they've done."

"Yes, well." Papa frowned. "We have come to see the few possessions they own returned to them. In particular, their clothing and a small tin from their parents. If you hand it over, I shall do all within my power to see your boat restored if it was not completely lost in the flood."

Grumbling, Mr. Simms slammed the door. From behind, Elizabeth could hear banging as contents were shuffled about. After a fairly long wait, he returned with a pile of clothing in his arms. Tossing it to the ground, Elizabeth and Jane scrambled to recover the shoes and garments.

Her arms full, Elizabeth snapped, "The tin, if you please?"

Grumbling some more, Mr. Simms stepped back inside. Moments later, he shoved a small container at her father.

Her papa said, "Sir, I shall see to replacing the boat you lost."

"The boat, new oars, and my gear I use for fishing."

Jane asked, "But are those not your oars leaning against your house?"

Affronted at the man's temerity, Elizabeth added, "I can confirm that there were no oars or fishing equipment inside the boat. You will get a boat and only a boat, one that is as old and rickety as was yours."

Her father mumbled as he tried to pry off the lid. "Let us see what we have here."

"Now, you see here." Mr. Simms wagged his finger at her at the same time the top popped off the tin.

Peering inside, the first thing Elizabeth saw was the impression on the paper where two round items no longer rested. "Pardon me, Mr. Simms, but where are the missing items? Do you still have them?"

"That coin is mine!" he insisted. "I brought them monsters from the ship and fed them while they was here." He pulled a ring from his pocket. "You can have this since it don't fit my hands."

As her father took the ring, Elizabeth said, "You received just compensation for the loss of the boat with the money you took from the children, Mr. Simms. Our business is concluded."

"But my boat? How am I supposed to fish without my boat?"

Elizabeth stepped closer. "Those children still bear the bruises you cruelly inflicted. They owe you nothing. We owe you nothing."

Stepping away from the smell surrounding the man and his residence, they returned to the carriage.

Once inside, her father chuckled, "If Ralph Simms had any intelligence, he would have given us the coin and kept the ring. It is a signet from a family known to me." He leaned across to show the face of the ring to his daughters. "I was at university with Mr. Ralph Simmons. We both had middling estates, an interest in literature, and little desire to move up in the world. His older brother held the family estate and already had several young sons. If I remember correctly, Briarwood is close to Bucklebury in Berkshire."

"What a lovely surprise for the children." Elizabeth was genuinely pleased.

During the mile journey, Elizabeth separated Rebekah's clothing from Jake's, while Jane folded them into neat piles. There was everything they would need for the winter. Examining the seam of one of the garments, Elizabeth noted that each stitch was evenly spaced and tight. They had been sewn by someone who dearly loved the children.

The relief on Jake's face when he saw the tin was palpable.

"Thank you very so much for getting this back, Mr. Bennet." Jake bowed formally. "Let's open it to see what Mama put inside."

"No, Jake," Rebekah insisted. "We need Mr. Darcy here before we can read it since he will know what is to be done."

"We need to find your family, Bekah." Elizabeth's attempt to reason with the little girl was rebuffed.

She immediately replied, "We need to find Mr. Darcy first." Rebekah glared; her arms folded across her chest.

Elizabeth knew that stance intimately since it was one that she saw reflected in her mirror when she was determined.

"Then I suggest that as soon as we get a break in the rain, you put on your coat, shoes, and stockings so we can go outside and look in the garden to see if we can find him."

"Yes!" The children dug through Jane's neat piles to select the garments they desired.

* * *

ELIZABETH STOOD at the edge of the shrubbery, peering into the distance as Jane chased the children around the garden. She understood the danger of exposure to the elements. She pictured Darcy in a comfortable cottage similar to the one Mr. and Mrs. Whitmer owned, possibly with a twisted ankle that did not allow him to walk. Or maybe he discovered someone else in troubled circumstances that desperately needed his help. Darcy would not overlook another's distress. What she refused to consider was him being close to water.

Was he, at that very moment, thinking of her with longing?

Her fingers toyed with the lace on her collar.

Stirring her resolve, Elizabeth returned her attention to the children.

CHAPTER 19

Colonel Fitzwilliam arrived at Longbourn early on the morning of the third day. His expression was grim.

"I need to procure a skiff to put into the river at the stone bridge where Darcy jumped. If he is holed up in a cave or amongst a tangle of debris along the riverbank, we will find him. As Bingley and Hurst observe the surroundings via boat, I will ride the riverbank again. If he is not found, my next destination is London, where my regiment will interview the mudlarkers to see if they plucked his pockets."

Elizabeth's hand covered her mouth, holding in her gasp.

The colonel's chin dipped to his chest. "I apologize, Miss Elizabeth, if I have shocked you. Bingley, Hurst, and the regiment saw no sign of Darcy. Not one person I interviewed has seen him on either side of the river." Rubbing his face, he sighed heavily. "I fear for Darcy's survival."

The pain in Elizabeth's chest threatened to drop her to her knees. She knew from her father's circulating papers of the mudlarkers, individuals who scoured the banks of the

Thames looking for treasures to sell from the debris, which often included the bodies of suicide or murder victims.

"No!"

"Miss Elizabeth, I am Darcy's closest friend and cousin. My deep affection for him has never blinded me to his character. You should know that he is stubborn to a fault. He would be here if there were any means humanly possible to survive. The only thing that could cause his continued absence was if he were physically unable."

Elizabeth tasted blood. Releasing the pressure of her fingers on her lips, she pleaded, "Colonel, I, too, know him to be a man of his word. He promised."

"I imagine he did." Stiffening his spine, Colonel Fitzwilliam said, "I spoke with Darcy's valet, Parker, who informed me that he has been in direct contact with the servants at the London house. Although I wished to keep this private, I asked Parker to inform me if word that his master showed up there. As of this morning, there was no word." He harrumphed. "He also mentioned that gossip of Darcy's situation has likely traveled across the square to my father's house. I cannot imagine either of my parents remaining in London long. It is likely they will rush north to see how they can take advantage."

With what she had been told of Lord Matlock, Elizabeth guessed the same. "His sister, Miss Darcy, knows of the danger?" Elizabeth's heart broke for the girl. To be orphaned and then hear it suggested that her only sibling was lost surely was devastating.

The colonel began pacing. "Gossip flows from one house to another in Town. With Parker's communication, I suspect that she does. Since I share guardianship of Miss Georgiana Darcy, who stands to inherit Pemberley, I will act to protect her. She is too young to discern who will attempt to curry favor for dishonest gain. With that in mind, I will tell you that one of Colonel Forster's officers is known to me. He is a reprobate and a rake. Once he heard Darcy was missing, I could see the greed in his eyes. I warned him that if he attempted to gain access to Darcy, Georgiana, or you, I would see him in an unmarked grave."

Elizabeth gasped. "Which officer?"

"George Wickham," the colonel sneered the name.

Lydia's favorite.

"Is he still with the local militia?"

"He is not." The colonel ran his hands through his hair. "Forster told me that Wickham was considering enlisting but had not yet done so. Once he was dismissed, the rogue was left with no money and no horse."

The implication of his words hit Elizabeth squarely in the chest. "That means he is still here. Is Mr. Darcy in danger from him?"

"One of my men is tracking every move Wickham makes. He is ordered to defend and protect should George get close. I will let nothing deter me from my task. I will search every inch of the stream and both sides of the river Lea. Once I reach the Thames, my regiment will cover every inch of the muddy banks. If Darcy is to be found, we will find him."

"I thank you." Even though she did not add the words, her eyes pleaded with him to bring him back safely.

Upon the colonel's departure, Elizabeth collapsed into a chair. Was she a fool for believing Darcy survived? Very likely. Nonetheless, being a fool in love was preferable to giving up, which she would not do until she heard from Colonel Fitzwilliam that all hope was lost.

When Rebekah arrived downstairs, she climbed up on Elizabeth's lap. As Elizabeth rocked the little girl back and forth, she drew strength from the skinny arms that encircled her.

"They will find him, my girl." The reassuring words soothed her own heart too.

* * *

DESPITE THE COOLNESS of the air, perspiration ran from Darcy's temples to his jaw. Although the river was an easy distance from where he stood, he would not go near the water. His throat was parched. He refused to consider whether his choice to leave Mr. Pierce's domicile was premature. His devotion to Elizabeth drew him forward.

He wished for a horse to cover the ground to his destination in minutes. Whether Darcy could hold himself erect in the saddle was another matter.

Through a force of will, he put one foot in front of the other.

He stumbled, falling to his knees. Pushing against the ground, he stood once again. Stepping around a tuft of earth, the toe of his boot caught on the edge of a stone sticking up from the mud. His other foot slipped, sending him back to the ground.

Determined to move forward, Darcy stood, wiping his filthy hands on his trousers. In the distance, a female apparition skipped, her long dark hair flowing behind her as her skirt twirled in the wind.

"Elizabeth!" he yelled. When she drifted away instead of moving closer, he tried again, this time, his voice was louder. "Come to me, dearest."

With an outstretched arm, her fingers wagged "goodbye."

"No!" He did not see the limb sticking out of the soil. This time, when he fell, he was unable to get up. His strength was depleted. "Elizabeth!"

* * *

As it was, matters developed exactly as Colonel Fitzwilliam supposed. Elizabeth was watching the children frolic in the garden, jumping from one puddle to the next, when two elegant coaches emblazoned with golden crests on the doors stopped in front of Longbourn. They were followed by several smaller carriages overburdened with luggage.

From within the first coach, a male voice barked orders. The equipage immediately behind contained a lady with an equally commanding tone.

Rushing the children inside to be taken up the stairs by Jane, Elizabeth attempted to calm her mother and younger sisters.

"Oh, my!" her mother fluttered. "It must be the Prince Regent himself come to call. Wait until I tell Lady Lucas who has come to Longbourn."

Lydia, Kitty, and Mary pressed their faces to the window, gawking.

Lydia sighed, "Look at that lace, Mama. Why, if that lady possessed half the bosom as mine, she would be better fit to be seen in public."

Kitty pushed. "Let me see."

Mary censured, "Lydia, ladies do not speak of bosoms in public unless it is with reference to being in the bosom of our Lord and Savior."

"Good god, Mary, but you are righteous." Lydia shoved the middle sister away from the window.

"Girls!" Instead of correcting the vulgarity of her youngest children, Francine Bennet wrangled her way to the glass. "Oh, my. Look at them!"

Wishing Darcy was by her side while grateful he was not, Elizabeth summoned her resolve. Seeing her family as Darcy's family would made her blush. Nevertheless, even though her mother and sisters acted silly, they were not mean-spirited.

Before their uninvited guests were ushered inside, Elizabeth hurried to her father.

"Lord Matlock is here."

Color drained from her father's face. "Here? At Longbourn? *Blast*! What am I to do?"

Elizabeth offered, "I do not suspect he is here to see you. Rather, his interest is in Mr. Darcy. However, I could be wrong." Hearing the front door opening, she added, "I must go, Papa."

Quickly returning to the drawing room, Elizabeth was standing next to the fireplace mantel, Darcy's favorite location when in company, as the newcomers entered.

The first entrant into the room demanded, "Cathy, would you see to Anne? She is sniveling again."

An older woman followed on his heels. "How dare you imply my child is in less than perfect health, Hugh. Why, if Darcy were alive, she would be mistress of Pemberley before summer. As it is, as the closest living relative, I shall take the estate under my authority until Anne learns all that is necessary to take charge of the house."

"You?" the man scoffed. "Not on your life will you be in charge of Pemberley. You barely manage Rosings Park. If not for Darcy and Richard, you would have bankrupted your property years ago."

"How dare you…"

Elizabeth cleared her throat, glancing in her mother's direction. When she discerned that Francine Bennet was overawed, she welcomed Lord Matlock and his family to Longbourn.

"Who are you?" Lord Matlock snapped, apparently irritated that Elizabeth interrupted his squabble.

Not one to be easily intimidated, yet aware that this man held her family's future in his purse, Elizabeth calmed herself before replying, "I am Miss Elizabeth Bennet. You are Lord Matlock?"

At the arch of her brow, his chin tilted arrogantly. "I am."

"Welcome to Longbourn, my lord. May I introduce my family?" Elizabeth waited for an introduction to the others.

He tilted his head toward the woman standing slightly behind him. "Lady Matlock. The loud one is my sister, Lady Catherine de Bourgh. The shy girl is Miss Darcy. The sickly one is my other niece, Anne."

A heavy-set younger man dressed in the garb of a parson loudly cleared his throat, insisting not to be overlooked.

"My sister's lackey is Carter. Or Commons. Or something."

"Collins, at your service, Lord Matlock." The parson practically scraped the floor with his bow. "My esteemed patroness, Lady Catherine, has—"

Lord Matlock turned his back on the clergyman and continued, speaking over the man, "We have heard an outrageous report that my nephew—"

"Our nephew!" insisted Lady Catherine.

"*My* nephew." Apparently, Lord Matlock was not one to be cowed by his sister. "Darcy disgracefully chose to end it all by jumping off a bridge. *Arrogant, irresponsible fool!*"

Elizabeth was stunned at the charge.

The girl, Miss Darcy, sobbed aloud as she stood alone and pitiful.

Rushing to her side, Elizabeth boldly clasped the girl's hand. Miss Darcy was shaking like a leaf. "Come." Leading her to a sofa, she said, "I beg you to be seated while I call for refreshments. Your journey has been long under trying circumstances."

Lord Matlock challenged, "What do you know of our circumstances?"

Unabashedly, Elizabeth replied, "My lord, when I last saw

Mr. Darcy after he rescued myself and two children from the river, he was alive and well."

Miss Darcy hiccupped. "Alive? My brother rescued you? He is alive?"

"Of course, he is not." Lady Catherine stated in no uncertain terms. "Once Darcy's body is located, we shall depart for Derbyshire to establish Anne as mistress, where she will set an example in womanly comportment for you to follow, Georgiana. When you marry, I will turn Pemberley into the property it was meant to be under my sister's hand."

Lord Matlock harrumphed. "Pemberley is mine!" Ignoring his sister, he added, "If anyone can find Darcy's lifeless body, it will be Richard. Now, tell me, Miss Bennet, where exactly were you when you saw my nephew?"

Patting Georgiana Darcy's hand, Elizabeth stepped away from the girl. "Mr. Darcy saw the three of us safely to a small farmer's cottage before departing for help from his friend, Mr. Bingley, at Netherfield Park. That was three days ago."

"Then, it is as I said. He has met with misfortune." Lord Matlock rubbed his hands together. "This is better news. Society frowns upon suicide. Either way, he is dead."

Elizabeth's spine stiffened. "My lord, I beg you not to give up hope."

Lord Matlock stepped closer. "Hope? Tell me, Miss Elizabeth, what do you *hope* to gain from Darcy's survival? What do you lose if he is not discovered to be alive? Are you claiming compromise, for I shall tell you now that you will gain none of Darcy's assets?"

"Compromise?" Francine Bennet squealed. "Lizzy, you said nothing, you sly girl. Why, I now suspect it was not those old cottagers who kept you warm that night but Mr. Darcy instead." She moved to Elizabeth's side. "Yes, we claim compromise, my lord."

Blood rushed to Elizabeth's face, heating her cheeks and

stirring her temper. Greed oozed from every pore of her mother's body. However, Francine Bennet was not the only one in the room who coveted what Darcy possessed.

Was that all Darcy was to his family? Was he under the illusion that they cared for him, or did he know he was merely a source of wealth?

They disgusted her.

Feeling a presence at her side, Elizabeth expected Jane when she looked. It was her father.

"Mrs. Bennet, you are to remove yourself and our daughters to your chambers." He did not blink until his wife acted on his command. Once the room was cleared, he continued, "Lord Matlock, my daughter is a lady from her head to her toes. If she says there was no compromise, then that is exactly what happened."

Lord Matlock sneered. "Who are you to speak to me, Bennet?"

The parson interrupted. "He is my father's cousin, Lord Matlock. Upon his death, this property is entailed to me. Therefore, as you are claiming Pemberley for yourself, I shall lay claim to this property in imitation of the brother of my esteemed patroness. Mr. Bennet's daughter, who immorally attempts to claim wealth from you based on a compromise, I shall take to task as I apply discipline to the proper degree."

Good heavens! That oaf would inherit Longbourn?

She shuddered before turning her attention away from the parson. Focusing on Mr. Darcy's uncle, she said, "Lord Matlock, I will not give up on Mr. Darcy easily. Rather than craving his possessions, my motive is a deep respect for his gentlemanlike conduct. He is the finest of men."

"How do I know you will not attempt a claim against his estate?"

"You doubt my word?" Fear at her boldness caused her heart to pound as moisture covered her palms.

"If you are to be believed, you will have your father put your promise in writing for all to witness." Lord Matlock's words dripped with ridicule. "Your father knows the value of a tightly written contract."

Her eyes pierced his as she lifted her chin. This man held the power of the nation in his palm, yet she did not fear him. Anger at his stubborn insistence of his nephew's demise for personal gain appalled her. Using terminology he would clearly understand, that of a predator to his prey, she stated, "I promise on my honor that I will make no attempt to entrap Mr. Fitzwilliam Darcy or his estate for any purpose if you forgive the debt owed by any Bennets or Longbourn. Do you agree?"

Had someone dropped a pin, it could have been heard in the silence.

The longer Lord Matlock took to reply, the quicker the blood raced through her veins until Elizabeth feared her head would explode.

"Done." Lord Matlock turned his back to her as if she were of little importance.

At that single word, her father collapsed onto the same sofa where Miss Darcy sat; his fingers pressed over his mouth.

"See here," Lady Catherine began, only to have her brother silence her.

"We are done here." Lord Matlock turned to leave. Stopping at the doorway, he looked back at Elizabeth. "You are a fool like the rest of your family, Miss Elizabeth. If you carry Darcy's progeny, even a bastard could make a claim against Pemberley. As it is, you will get nothing."

Smoothing her hands on her skirt, Elizabeth replied, "Believe as you will, Lord Matlock. However, before you go, I shall write out our agreement for you and Father to sign."

"Very well." He waved her off, then turned to stare out the window, ignoring the rest of the room.

Elizabeth sat at the writing table in the corner. Within moments, she was sanding the document.

Lord Matlock barely glanced at the paper before penning his signature. Her father, who waited until Hugh Fitzwilliam had stepped back, also signed. Not wanting to be left out, Lady Catherine insisted upon adding her signature.

"Come, Georgie," Lord Matlock ordered. "To Pemberley."

Barely waiting until the carriages were loaded and gone, Elizabeth dropped onto the sofa where Miss Darcy had sat. She wanted to laugh and cry at the same time. In truth, Elizabeth had bilked Lord Matlock with the deal she made, for her character would never allow her to entrap a gentleman under any circumstances. She would prey on no man, especially one she loved. What was common conduct in his world was unknown in hers.

Unbeknownst to Lord Matlock and Lady Catherine, on Darcy's return, she would not chase after him or pursue him. She would not need to. They would meet as one, walking side by side for the rest of their lives.

Once he returned.

CHAPTER 20

Colonel Richard Fitzwilliam tapped his heels against Excalibur's flanks. The horse responded immediately by lunging up the hill. Despite the narrow path, the animal navigated the uneven ground with ease. Topping the rise, the colonel drew his spyglass from its leather holder.

To the right were small parcels where tenant farmers toiled. Sweeping toward his left, he saw where trails and roads crisscrossed the landscape. He stopped his motion, moving the spyglass back. Before him unfolded a scene he had seen a hundred times on the battlefield—a man was stripping a downed soldier of all his worldly possessions. The victim was flat on his back, making the task of the thief easy.

Wait! Dark wavy hair topped a long torso and legs. Darcy?

Grinding his heels into his mount, Richard rode like the hounds of hell were nipping at his boots. Pulling his pistol from his waistband, he aimed it at the poor bloke who would soon breathe his last.

They were almost on him when the perpetrator heard the hoofbeats. Standing, the thief drew his own pistol.

Blast and damnation! It was Wickham.

With a whistle, the colonel drew Excalibur to a stop.

Pointing the barrel of his weapon right between wily Wickham's ribs, Richard snarled. "You dare to steal from Darcy? You dare to draw on me?"

Wickham carelessly shrugged, although the hand holding the pistol shook slightly. "A man has to do what a man has to do."

"Well, you see, Wickham, that is the point, is it not? You have little of a real man about you. The rest of you is nothing but a rabid mongrel."

Wickham's body stiffened as his arm raised by an inch.

Richard knew the signs. As he squeezed the trigger, Excalibur shifted his weight to his other leg, causing his aim to go wide. Instead of shooting the gun out of Wickham's hand, the bullet pierced the rake's heart.

"Blast you, Richard!" Wickham collapsed next to Darcy.

The colonel paid Wickham no mind. Instead, he rushed to Darcy, kneeling on the ground to press his ear to his cousin's chest. The rise and fall were shallow. That Darcy had not stirred from the gunfire testified to his illness.

"Help me!" Richard yelled into the wind. "I need help now."

Grabbing his horse's reins, he pulled him close to where his cousin lay. "Whoa." His well-trained animal would not move.

A man with young men running behind him hurried toward Richard.

Seeing two men on the ground, one with blood pooling at his side, the farmer stopped.

"What is happening here?"

"I came upon this thief stealing from this gentleman, who happens to be my cousin. The one I need help with is ill. The other can rot on the ground as far as I am concerned."

With a nod, the man and his two boys helped Darcy to stand until he leaned against the horse. Richard mounted behind the saddle, guiding Darcy until his cousin rested in front of him, leaning against his chest.

He dug in his saddle bags for the few coins he always carried. Tossing them to the men, he said, "I thank you kindly."

"What do we do with him?" The farmer gestured to Wickham.

"Do as you please. He was willing to take advantage of an innocent man instead of coming to the aid of someone in need. He gets nothing more from me."

Turning Excalibur toward Longbourn, he tightened his grip on his cousin and rode due west.

* * *

A RESTLESS FEELING grew inside Elizabeth until she could no longer remain at Longbourn. Her father had returned to his bookroom with a much lighter step. Her mother and three younger sisters hurried to Lucas Lodge to boast about their guests. Jane was in the garden with Jake and Rebekah.

Tying her bonnet ribbons under her chin, Elizabeth studied her face in the mirror. She looked wretched. So much about her had changed since she walked to the bridge that day. She fretted about the future of her and her family.

Departing her home, she wandered toward Meryton.

An epiphany of sorts hit her before she exited the boxwood-lined walkway.

Since his father's death, Darcy had to stand against his forceful uncle and aunt. Had anyone stood beside him? For a certainty, Colonel Fitzwilliam was loyal to his cousin. But was he always available? The answer was easy. He was not.

Had his sister actively supported her brother? Again, the answer was simple. Miss Darcy was far too timid.

What of her? Who stood with her efforts to rally against the silliness of her family that her father ridiculed? Did Jane? Not really. Instead of supporting change, Jane excused bad conduct out of misguided love.

Elizabeth huffed. In essence, like Darcy, Elizabeth was on her own.

Was this a bad thing? She could not help but think it was not since it formed key elements of their characters. Perhaps it was why they were drawn to each other, that recognition that the other was capable enough to be alone while at the same time desirous of a companion who valued their nature.

Reaching up to pull a twig from an overhanging branch, she snapped it into as many small pieces as she was able.

Approaching the bridge, Elizabeth was grateful when no boat carrying two young vagabonds came out from underneath. Instead, she leaned over the stone parapet, dropping the twigs into the water to watch them float away.

She wished with all her being to see the gentleman strolling toward her, his hand reaching out to entwine his fingers with her own. Her arms ached to hold him. Elizabeth wanted him beside her with a passion that threatened to crush her from its weight. Her heart yearned for him. Without him, she was incomplete.

Where are you, Fitzwilliam Darcy? Please, please come back to me.

Swiping the tears from her cheeks with impatient hands, Elizabeth began walking along the river to where the dam had been. The earth was scarred and ugly. Climbing her way up the hillside, she cautiously stepped along the tracks where Mr. Whitmer's cart dug furrows into the soil. Pressing forward, she reached Netherfield Park. Following the pathway to the river, she stood in the exact spot where Darcy found her on the day she escaped from Caroline Bingley's insults. She recalled the conversation where he revealed that he tried to rescue her from her failed trip to the Amazon. She smiled at the memory. Fitzwilliam Darcy was twice her hero.

Oh, but she wanted him to be safe.

Looking toward the river Lea, she saw nothing out of order until she spotted a horse approaching from the east.

It was…it was the colonel's horse?

Her breath caught.

Yes, and there were… *Oh, my good heavens!*

Elizabeth ran until her lungs threatened to burst.

* * *

DARCY COULD NOT RECALL when he became conscious he was on a horse with his cousin. They had not ridden like that since they were children.

"Rich?" he whispered, his throat on fire.

"Yes, Darcy?"

His neck felt too weak to support the weight of his head. His chest and back were warm where Richard had draped his great coat around him. Darcy wiggled his toes. His boots were gone.

"Thirsty."

"I suppose you are." His cousin leaned forward. With some effort, a canteen was provided with the lid already open. "Here, I'll tip it up."

The first drops were too cold on Darcy's tongue. The next swallow was perfect. Unfortunately, Richard would not let him have any more.

"Little by little, Cousin."

Darcy leaned back, refusing to be embarrassed by his inability to support himself.

"We are almost to Netherfield, which means a bath and a

bed for you. If Bingley's cook is any good, she will have a pot of broth ready to serve."

Darcy had no desire to see Bingley. "Elizabeth."

"She is quite a woman, Darce."

He could feel every word his cousin uttered at his back. "Yes."

"In fact, if she was not completely devoted to you, I think—"

"Richard, shut up."

His cousin chuckled.

Richard stiffened, suddenly alert. Looking around, Darcy noted nothing out of the ordinary except—

His heart shot to his throat. His arms flexed. His legs instinctively tightened around the girth of the horse.

"Elizabeth!" Leaning forward, he clutched the mane in his fists, hanging on for his life.

Richard kicked Excalibur into motion, shortening the distance. Before they came to a stop, his Elizabeth was there, clutching his knee, her head resting on his thigh.

With Richard's help, he slid from the horse into her arms. Mustering every ounce of strength, he pulled her to him, her temple on his shoulder, her face pressed into his neck.

"I love you, Elizabeth, with my heart and soul. You have seen me at the height of arrogance and as I am now, in the garments of a farmer without a penny or a shoe to my name. Will you take me as I am? Will you have me as a husband?"

She laughed as her tears soaked his skin.

"Yes, my wonderful man. I want you exactly as you are."

He kissed her temple, then her cheek. When she boldly rested her palms on the sides of his face, pulling him toward her, he kissed her with the recognition that he was finally home.

* * *

When Darcy was helped to his bedchamber, Parker was ready with a tray of food and a hot bath. Miss Bingley insisted on providing everything Darcy desired. He somehow doubted his request to have Elizabeth see to his needs would have met with her approval.

"Sir, it is good to have you back." Parker fussed. "Mr. Bingley and your cousin have been tireless in their search. According to them both, Miss Elizabeth was a source of constant encouragement, never once having her confidence in your safe return diminished."

Darcy drank deeply of the cool water his valet provided. "Then you should know that she will soon be my wife." Joy shot through him as he said it.

"Very good, sir. Pemberley will benefit, as will you." Bowing, Parker moved to leave the room.

Darcy's body ached, and he was weaker than a newborn babe. Yet, he was happier than he had ever been.

"See to my cousin, I beg you. Bingley has his family and his servants to care for him. Richard does not."

"I will be pleased to be of service, sir."

No sooner had his valet stepped through the door than his cousin entered, making himself comfortable in the chair next to the bed.

"Yes?" Darcy asked, seeing that something weighty was pressing down on his cousin.

After a long pause, Richard sat back in the chair, staring at the ceiling.

"Your Elizabeth told me Father and Aunt Catherine were at Longbourn this morning. They had Georgie with them. Once Elizabeth promised not to entrap you in exchange for the release of Mr. Bennet from an egregious debt, they departed for Pemberley to lay claim to your estate."

"Let them."

"What?" Richard sat up. "You will allow them to encroach on your property?"

Darcy grinned. "I will. Richard, I was pulled from the river by a man your father ruined. Had not Elizabeth bargained for her family, her father would have been tossed into Marshalsea, likely in the coming days. There are many others I learned. I no longer have pride in being family to an earl. Your father and his imperious sister are a plague. I choose honor and loyalty above relatives whose conduct is worse than the most disgusting criminal element in England. As to the matter of Elizabeth, she could never 'entrap' me since I willfully and joyfully enter any cage or lair she creates."

"What are you planning?" Richard leaned forward, eager for justice. "Before you continue, you should know that Wickham aimed to kill me."

"Wickham? Where did you see him? No, ignore my question. I do not want to know. I see that his efforts were not successful. Where is he?"

"Dead."

Regret for a life wasted threatened. His former friend was in every way reprehensible; Darcy's father would have mourned the loss of the man he thought Wickham to be. Only Richard and Darcy knew Wickham had never been a gentleman.

"Richard, I have a plan that might work. With your help, I think we can tie your father's and aunt Catherine's hands so tightly they will never again be able to creep into someone else's pockets."

"I'm in." Richard volunteered.

"Let me tell you what I have in mind."

CHAPTER 21

*E*lizabeth sat alone in the front drawing room, overcome with concern for Darcy. Occasionally, one of Netherfield's servants would ask if she required anything. When the clock chimed the hour, Mr. and Mrs. Hurst meandered into the room, closely followed by Miss Bingley. For the better part of an hour, they ignored Elizabeth's presence. She was rather pleased with the arrangement.

Finally, upon descending the grand staircase, Mr. Bingley approached Elizabeth. Failing to acknowledge his sister's demand for the latest information concerning their guest, he addressed Elizabeth. "I have sent for the local apothecary. Darcy refused to have his physician brought from London. If you do not mind, Miss Elizabeth, I would happily carry a note to Longbourn for Miss Bennet to join you. That is, if you would like her company?"

What a kind-hearted, self-sacrificing man! He will be good for Jane.

"I certainly do not mind, although I shall only remain

until I hear a report that Mr. Darcy is making good progress with his recovery. Then, I am needed at Longbourn."

Miss Bingley scoffed. "Why would you believe Mr. Darcy would report to you, Eliza Bennet? You are not family. Nor are you a particularly close friend. Why, in all my association with the family, I do not recall Miss Georgiana Darcy ever mentioning you as an acquaintance."

Elizabeth remained silent. To react would feed Miss Bingley's self-importance. Instead, Elizabeth caught Miss Bingley's eye, then deliberately looked away.

The lady must have felt the sting since she added, "The only thing that would bring dear Georgiana to Hertfordshire is her brother. Since his arrival several weeks ago, he chose not to have her come to Netherfield Park. You see, she is used to the highest ranks of society."

The colonel's voice came from the doorway. He glared at Miss Bingley.

"I understand that my family was at Longbourn this morning. As is usual, Miss Darcy accompanied my parents and my aunt, Lady Catherine." Turning his attention to Elizabeth, he added, "Did you find my young cousin well, Miss Elizabeth?"

"Distressed from anxiety over her brother, but well." She wanted to chuckle. The startled expression on Miss Bingley's face was not an appealing look for her.

Color rose in Miss Bingley's cheeks. "Lord and Lady Matlock were at Longbourn? Well, I never!"

"I imagine not," the colonel quipped. "Say, Bingley, before you ride to Longbourn, I have an express to my brother that needs to be delivered today. Would you carry it to Meryton for London?"

Miss Bingley's full attention was given to the request. "Your brother? Viscount Smithton? You will invite him to Netherfield Park?"

The colonel bowed. "If it meets with your brother's approval."

Before Mr. Bingley could utter a word, his sister stated unequivocally, "For a certainty, the viscount would be a welcome guest. I shall have the servants prepare a suite immediately."

Miss Bingley glared at Elizabeth, who had no difficulty capturing her meaning. Miss Bingley did not want any Bennets at Netherfield Park.

"Bingley, is this acceptable to you? Freddy is never entirely comfortable in the country, but I am sure he will mind his manners, for the most part." Colonel Fitzwilliam added.

The colonel handed a letter to Mr. Bingley, and the room cleared but for Elizabeth and the colonel.

"Please, tell me if your cousin needs anything I am able to provide."

The slight lift at the corner of his mouth preceded his reply. "I believe you are everything my cousin needs, Miss Elizabeth. I do, however, have a request of my own."

"How might I be of service?" As each second passed, during which he failed to reply, her anxiety increased. Finally, he nodded as if he were now certain of his course.

"Darcy told me that my father has taken advantage of yours. Do you know if he still has the artifact that was sold to him?"

"The map of Peru?"

"Yes. Before you agree to approach your father, you should know that once it leaves my hands, it will not be able to be returned."

"I see." She considered his request. "You have a plan, I suspect."

"Darcy does."

"Then it will be one where a measure of justice will be

gained for those who have been bilked, I suppose." At the colonel's nod, she continued. "Are you certain it is a wise course to alienate your family to satisfy those unrelated to you? What will you gain? Sir, should you pursue this, though honorable, the cost to you would be high. I will not pretend to know your circumstances, but is it an expense you can safely bear?"

He shook his head. "I should have known."

"Known what?" Elizabeth could not stop herself from asking. Richard Fitzwilliam gave the appearance that any time he would jump into action. She doubted he ever fully relaxed. Perhaps it was because of his chosen career. Whatever the case, the fact that Darcy trusted him implicitly meant that she could too.

"My cousin reacted exactly the same as you." He grinned, then sobered. "Although I do not believe that sons need to pay for the sins of their fathers, often that is the case. In the distant future, my dream of settling on a small property to raise quality horseflesh with my own family at my side will suffer if something is not done to put a leash on my father and older brother. This dream has sustained me through challenging times. If I do nothing, I will never have peace."

Her heart ached for him. Unabashedly, she declared, "From the little your cousin told me, he, too, has little peace due to the actions and attitudes of his father. The pressure my father placed on his family by a single poor decision threatened to ruin my dreams. I will not discourage you from acting, Colonel. I only ask that you listen to the wise counsel you received in your cousin's chambers."

"I will." He stood to leave. "To reassure you, Darcy is a bear of a patient, but I have no doubt he will survive. Whatever trials you suffered together have given him the will to live and the hope of future happiness. I am forever in your debt."

"Colonel." Elizabeth moved to stand directly in front of him. "You no doubt realize that to act against the mighty Lord Matlock, comrade of the prince, your career could suddenly end. At the same time, you would pursue this course and gain the loyalty of men like my father, who would do whatever is within their power to come to your aid. This is a path both Mr. Darcy and I can fully support."

"I thank you, Miss Elizabeth. I look forward to welcoming you to the family, such as we are."

With a clipped salute, he departed Netherfield Park.

Before Elizabeth reached the window to see the colonel mount Excalibur to ride away, an older man peeked inside the drawing room, catching her attention.

"Miss Elizabeth," he whispered. "I beg your pardon. I am Parker, valet to Mr. Darcy. I fear he will not rest until he sees you. I would hope you would see fit to accompany me upstairs."

Without a word or a moment of hesitation, she followed him.

* * *

"Elizabeth," he sighed her name, igniting a fire in her heart.

Approaching the bed, she clasped his hand in hers. A slight tug from him was all it took for her to join him. Her forehead brushed his cheek, feeling the heat radiating from his skin before settling in that soft spot under his ear. His arms tightened around her, drawing her closer.

He smelled of shaving soap and sunshine.

"I miss your whiskers, Fitzwilliam." Her fingers tapped his chin. "However, I am entirely grateful for Parker's care of you. Are you doing as he insists?"

She felt the rumble of Darcy's chuckle against the hand she had moved to his chest.

"For the most part," Darcy admitted. His sigh was heavy. "Did you see Richard?"

"I did. He left for Longbourn after briefly outlining his intent. Will he be well?"

"My cousin is not dependent on Lord Matlock for his expenses. His mother brought a small estate to the marriage designated for the second son, so Richard would always have a home. Stanton Hall is but ten miles from Pemberley. My steward oversees the care of the property."

"This is a comfort to know. He risks much."

Darcy entwined his fingers with hers. "His brother Freddy is a pompous fool who has a lifetime of bringing reproach against his father's house by gambling far above his ability. Then, he panders to Uncle Hugh until he is forgiven. It is this propensity that Richard will use. As I recover my strength, he will contact as many individuals as possible that he knows who have been abused by his father. Offering all the items he is able to gain to Freddy as genuine, Freddy will gratefully dispose of whatever funds my uncle has made available to him to curry favor."

"Why, this is brilliant! Viscount Smithton will use Lord Matlock's own money to purchase relief for those who have been poorly used. Will it be enough to put your uncle on notice that he needs to change his course?"

Darcy nodded. "Freddy let it slip that his father was bold enough to sell counterfeit statues to Prinny himself. Once the Prince Regent learns that his compatriot duped him, Uncle Hugh will be knocked off his self-exalted perch."

"Oh, but this is good," Elizabeth admitted. "A brilliant plan from the mind of a brilliant man."

"You think I am brilliant?" Darcy hesitantly inquired.

She leaned up to look him in the eye. "I think you are both wise and kind. I think that when you love, you do so from the fullness of your heart. Other men pale against you to the point I do not notice their existence at all. Because of this, I look forward to all we will learn from each other in the years to come. You are the best of men, Fitzwilliam, and nothing or no one will ever convince me otherwise."

He kissed her forehead, holding his lips at that spot for the longest time. Finally, he whispered against her skin, "Thank you. I love you now, Elizabeth, and I suspect our love will grow each day."

She smiled, his beautiful words soothing her heart. "Then let us forge our own path to happiness, bringing your sister along with us until she sees a sterling example of what a true marriage should be."

"Do you love me?" he asked, his voice hesitant.

"I unequivocally, irrevocably, unquestionably love you, Fitzwilliam Darcy."

She kissed him, pouring her heart and soul into the touch of their lips, sealing her words with the promise of so much more.

Parker and a maid violently cleared their throats. Acting immediately, Elizabeth jumped up, returning to the chair next to Darcy's bed, smoothing her hair, and straightening her shoulders. Glancing over to find a mischievous grin on Darcy's face, she loved him even more.

She mouthed, "You are impossible, sir."

His smile widened. "You are too."

It was then she heard a rap on the door.

"Mr. Darcy's mail, sir." Parker held a massive stack of letters in both his hands. Quite a few of them were rimmed in black.

His brow furrowed in question; Darcy struggled to sit against the headboard. "I suppose that news of my demise has spread through London."

Elizabeth's gaze shot to him. She reached out to stroke his arm, making sure, again, that he was alive and present.

In less than a moment, Darcy had the mail sorted into three piles, those letters rimmed in black the tallest stack. Selecting one, Darcy broke the seal, gave it a cursory glance, then handed it to Elizabeth. "Please read this aloud, if you would?"

Taking the paper from him, she easily envisioned them doing this daily for the next sixty years, sharing the news and discussing possible outcomes. She rejoiced at the prospect. Then, she read the letter.

My dear Miss Darcy,

We were shocked to hear of the passing of your brother. He was reputed to be a fine man. As a kindness and to ease your distress, we offer the support of our eldest son, Mr. Harold Mortensen, an intelligent, handsome gentleman known to your uncle, Lord Matlock. When you are available, we plan to call upon you to offer our sympathies in person.

Respectfully sharing in your sorrows,

The Right Honorable Lord and Lady Mortensen

Elizabeth threw the offensive letter on his lap as if the words burned her fingers. "How dare they!"

Darcy brushed the letter aside. "Many will dare. They see Georgiana as vulnerable and ripe for the picking."

"Will they not be surprised when we ride into London with happy faces."

He harrumphed. "We are far more formidable than any who attempt to gain access to Pemberley through my sister."

"I love you, Fitzwilliam." She squeezed his hand. "In better news, I will share that Father, Jane, and I approached Mr. Ralph Simms about the possessions belonging to Jake and Rebekah. We were surprised to discover the tin was still in his possession. Although whatever money was inside was gone, there was a ring with the Simmons family crest that Papa recognized as belonging to a former schoolmate. We are awaiting news from Mr. Ralph Simmons of Briarwood in Berkshire."

"This is good news indeed." Darcy took both her hands in his. "Will you remain at Netherfield Park as long as you are able?"

"I cannot. I fear that Mr. Bingley will capture all of Jane's attention, leaving the twins without entertainment or purpose. They need me."

"I need you too. Nevertheless, we will only have them with us until they are reunited with their family. We will have each other forever."

Before they were disturbed again, they shared another kiss. Then another. Then another.

CHAPTER 22

Over the next week, Darcy drank every drop of broth, took every vile drop of medicine, and ate every bite of dry toast to recover his strength. Despite Parker's fussing, throughout each day, he counted to three hundred and then attempted to stand. The knot at the back of his skull finally started to shrink, making the steps he tried to take more stable as the world began to level.

Letters of sympathy continued to arrive with regularity. Once the missives of true friends were separated from those seeking to improve their status at his expense, Darcy was surprised to learn how many families were not self-serving. Those who begged for the opportunity to worm their way into the Darcy family coffers would be shunned. The others would always be welcomed to Pemberley.

Bingley had never heard from Lord Matlock or Lady Catherine, asking for news of Darcy. Parker had intercepted three letters from Caroline Bingley to Georgiana, where she likely meant to share the news of Darcy's survival and rescue. Darcy held them in his chambers. While he loathed the idea of his sister believing him to be lost to her, Richard needed time to implement the plan to bring Lord Matlock to his knees.

Daily, Elizabeth either walked or rode the pony cart to Netherfield. The few stolen moments he saw her were always with others around. He was desperate to be in her company again, where they had privacy.

Many times, he pondered the differences between him and his uncle. Darcy's love for Elizabeth meant he would do anything for her. Were he a poor man, Darcy knew enough about himself to be confident he would work hard for his family. Never would he break or bend the law to grasp something that did not belong to him. Elizabeth was the same. Her dignity and honor would never have her reaching for something, not hers. Hugh Fitzwilliam's love of money meant he would do anything for more.

On the eighth day, Darcy was able to descend the stairs without gasping for air. He was pleased to be welcomed by the sight of Elizabeth and Miss Bennet sitting on the sofa with Jake and Rebekah between them. The Hursts and Miss Bingley were at the other end of the room.

Bingley, standing next to where Miss Bennet sat, saw him first.

"Darcy! Well done. It is wonderful to have you join us."

"Thank you, Bingley. The effort was worth the wait."

Miss Bingley noted, "Mr. Darcy, surely it would be better for your recovery to enjoy the quiet of our family alone. Perhaps our guests can return at another time?"

"Caroline!" Bingley snapped.

"Contrary to your opinion, Miss Bingley, I am delighted to see your guests."

To Jake and Rebekah, he extended his hands. Without hesitation, Rebekah ran to him, launching herself into his arms.

Hugging the girl, he spun her in circles. "I have missed

you, Miss Bekah." When he stopped, Jake was at his side. "And you, young man, look like you have grown at least an inch or two. Have you been eating your way from one end of the Bennets' larder to the other, or are your shoes making you tall?"

The lad replied, "Mr. Darcy, I've got to tell you that Cook is just about the finest woman alive. She makes what she calls scones with bits of fruit and nuts that tastes better than anything I've ever eaten. Why, look!" He pulled his bottom lip down. "I lost my first tooth on one of those nuts. That means I'm getting bigger."

Forever in competition with her brother, Rebekah pulled down her bottom lip. "I still have all my teeth."

He hugged her again before setting her back on her feet.

"You both are growing."

The little girl wrapped her fingers around two of his, tugging until he was seated next to Elizabeth. With Jake on one side and Bekah on his lap, Miss Bennet moved to another chair.

The little girl said, "Mr. Darcy, our Simmons family is coming tomorrow to get us. They sent a letter that Miss Jane read that said they were sad because they wanted children in their house but didn't have any. They especially like twins, they said. They have new puppies and a black kitten with white paws named Fluffy."

"Yeah, and Mr. Ralph Simmons said he already loves us even though he hasn't seen us yet. I asked Mr. Bennet to write back that we have the tin. Bekah wants you to look at it first. I brought it with me in case you want to see inside."

Every inch of the boy's countenance was vulnerable.

Darcy said, "I would like nothing more."

Elizabeth said, "They waited to be in your presence to have the letters read. Not even my father has seen everything inside."

"Then let us read them now."

He opened the container and unfolded the parchment. Clearing his throat, he read:

30 October 1809

Dear family,

I will begin with an apology for the great length of time that has passed since departing Briarwood. I do hope this finds the family well. Are the last of the Simmons brood remaining at home? Are Millicent and Arnold staying out of mischief? Surely, they have reached the age to leave the care of their governess and tutor. Has Matthew taken a wife? Has Beatrice yet presented Ralph with an heir and a spare? Father, have you recovered from the loss of our mother, finding happiness if possible? It is my hope that all remaining in the family are prospering.

From the moment my ship landed in Philadelphia, the excitement and possibilities for a healthy young gentleman kept me occupied from daylight to dawn. Opportunities for advancement are around every corner, even for a third son.

I was not long in America before I met Miss Abigail Church. She is the loveliest of women with a kind nature who knows the value of hard work. My wife is quiet and private, unlike myself. Her love gives me peace and comfort.

On June 20, 1804, in our parish church at Potter County, Pennsylvania, we wed. On September 2, 1806, we were delivered of two children, Rebekah Joy and Jacob Stephen. They are healthy twins whose looks favor their mother more than they do my own. I am grateful this is so.

My journey led to another discovery, which I am confident will surprise you. Even though I loathed university, in helping my wife increase her education, I learned that I love to teach. Being an educator was never my intention, yet the small school where I instruct the children of others along with my own fills me with daily reasons for happiness. There are seventeen students ranging from aged three (my own) to fifteen. Each learns at their own pace. Seeing them make progress gives me a sense of purpose.

Dear ones, if this letter has come into your possession, then something dire has happened. Abigail and I have discussed at length the importance of our children coming to know their heritage. Therefore, I shall write you a separate letter to be posted immediately with my greetings and the information with which I began this missive. Now that I am no longer here to speak for myself, I will share with you my greatest hopes.

My wife is tasked with delivering herself and our children to Briarwood. Please use the enclosed items to see to their future. It is not much, but it will give them a start. I pray you welcome them into the home of my youth. Care for them. If you are able, love them. They are the best of me. Wishing you a long life and continued success,

Your son and brother,

Mr. Stephen Ralph Simmons

Darcy held the paper closer. "There is a note written in graphite at the bottom. "It says:"

I, Abigail Simmons, am unwell. I fear I will not survive to see England. Please, I beg you, see my children to my husband's family in Bucklebury. Remind Jacob and Rebekah that they are loved.

Mrs. Stephen Simmons

The poor woman! To leave the country of her birth to approach strangers to care for her children spoke of a devotion to family that was unparalleled.

Jake asked, "What do you think? It's a pretty good letter, isn't it?"

Reaching around the lad to pull him close, Darcy replied, "I find this letter excellently done. Your father was both educated and responsible. Your mother's love is unquestionable. Had your parents lived, you would have had a good family. As it is, the relaxed way he writes to his father about his brothers and sister indicates that his family is kind. The penmanship is clearly legible, and the direction for your care is sound. I do not believe I have ever read a finer letter."

Jake nodded once, then announced, "It's a good thing they are coming for us since it sounds like they need some children to play with those puppies."

"And the cat," Rebekah added.

Darcy pulled Rebekah closer. He would miss the twins. From the tender look on Elizabeth's face, so would she.

An image of them in the private sitting room connecting the master's and mistress's suites at Pemberley while entertaining their future children flashed across his mind. The scene was welcoming and comforting.

Determined to see his responsibility through, Darcy announced, "I plan to be at Longbourn tomorrow when the Simmons family arrives to ensure they will take great care of a boy who likes big dogs named Max and a girl who favors the color pink."

"And if they don't?" Jake asked, his eyes wide open, the knuckles of his fingers white.

"Well, that depends. Without a doubt, they will love you, so that is not a problem. What I am willing to do is negotiate terms should they only like small dogs or green. Do you think you could come to an agreement to live with them in peace under those dire circumstances?"

Rebekah chuckled. "You are silly, Mr. Darcy."

"Me? Silly?" He grinned.

Jake said, "Then I'm happy you are coming."

Darcy teased, "Do you think Miss Elizabeth wants me there?"

He loved the roses that bloomed in her cheeks at his outlandish question.

"Yes!" Both children proclaimed.

"Do you want me there?" he asked her slyly, already knowing her answer.

"I do," she replied, her smile brightening the room more than a thousand lit candles.

Miss Bingley said, "I cannot think the journey would be good for you, sir. Three miles across muddy trails to meet strangers you will likely never see again will not serve you well. Better it would be for you to remain here where you will be cared for by those who are devoted to you."

Darcy's brow arched. "There is no one more devoted to me than Miss Elizabeth. As my betrothed, I am confident she will provide the best care possible."

"Betrothed?" Miss Bingley's hand flew to her chest, the color rushing from her face. "You offered for her?" she shrieked.

"I have not spoken with Mr. Bennet yet, but we will wed." He stood, holding his available hand out to Elizabeth. "I believe it is incumbent upon me to rectify my oversight. To Longbourn."

She smiled, accepting his hand. "To Longbourn."

CHAPTER 23

By day's end, her father accepted Darcy's offer for Elizabeth and Bingley's offer for Jane.

After the initial shock of learning that wealthy men would be marrying her two eldest, Francine Bennet began planning a wedding breakfast suitable to entertain the whole shire.

Darcy interrupted her. "I beg your pardon, Mrs. Bennet, but Elizabeth and I will marry before the Simmons family arrives tomorrow. We want the children to witness the ceremony."

"Who are the Simmons family to us? What of Lord Matlock and Lady Catherine de Bourgh? What of your sister and the handsome colonel? Do you not want them here instead?"

Without thinking, he replied, "I do regret not having my sister and the colonel here, but they will both understand our necessity of marrying right away."

He could have bitten his tongue off for his poor phrasing. As it was, Mrs. Bennet dropped into the nearest chair, her handkerchief fluttering to fan her heated face.

"My Lizzy? You two…?"

Darcy hurried to explain. "We did nothing untoward. We were, however, together long enough to cause tongues to wag. I will not have reproach brought against us that might make it a challenge for you to find husbands for your remaining daughters. Additionally, we almost died. I will not waste another day without her."

"I see. Yes, well…it was an easy misunderstanding to make." Her relief was palpable.

Elizabeth added, "Besides, Mama, this means you will not need to bear the expense of my wedding clothes or for additional guests at the wedding breakfast. You can gift Jane everything you had set aside for my wedding or as much as Papa allows."

Elizabeth's words moved her mother to act. Leaving the room without excusing herself, she charged into Mr. Bennet's study.

The youngest Bennet girl pouted. "I wanted to be the first to marry."

Jake must have heard her because he offered, "Well, I'm available if you want. You've got to like big dogs, though, and you must have Cook teach you to make them scones."

Lydia had the grace to smile at the lad, treating his offer sincerely.

She said, "I do suppose that by the time I waited until you were taller than me, you will think me too advanced in years. I do appreciate the offer."

He shrugged, then joined his sister at the toy basket that had been brought from the nursery during their stay.

Darcy would miss Jake and Rebekah very much.

* * *

THE NEXT DAY, Darcy and Bingley arrived at the *White Stag* inn, where their valets had their finest suits pressed and brushed.

Bingley said, "It is deuced difficult not having road access from Netherfield Park to here. After discussing the matter with Jane, I think the best solution is to look for an estate closer to Pemberley we can purchase. This will put us within easy distance so the sisters can see each other often."

Darcy was pleased. "By the time you marry in June, you will have less than three months left of your lease. Should you spend your wedding trip at Pemberley, Elizabeth and I could help you find something that meets your needs and desires."

Bingley pulled at his cuffs, seemingly more nervous than the groom-to-be. "Caroline has agreed to stay with the Hursts at my townhouse in Town. They are not welcome to join us on our wedding tour." He shuddered.

Darcy could never imagine having company in the house on his wedding night. He wanted the start of his marriage to Elizabeth to be private and undisturbed.

A knock pounded on the door.

"Enter," Darcy said distractedly, still thinking about Elizabeth and the night to come.

Richard burst through the door, immediately followed by Jake.

"Where is Parker?" Richard asked, stepping aside so Darcy had a clear view of Jake. The lad was a mess. "The Simmons family arrived with a monster of a dog with enough long hair for three animals. As you can see, the animal tried to bathe the boy with his tongue. He is a bit worse for wear."

It took several long minutes for his valet to clean up Jake Simmons.

"Richard, I am delighted you are here." Darcy had written

of his plans the afternoon prior. "Bingley offered to stand up with me if you could not. However, I was afraid all his attention would be on Miss Bennet, and he would forget to bring the rings."

Bingley honestly admitted, "It is possible."

Richard cleared his throat, "Before you came to Hertfordshire, I left you to find happiness. I admit to you now that you did well, Cousin. Elizabeth will be the making of you."

"She will," Darcy admitted, grinning like a fool. "Let us be on our way. I am ready to marry my bride."

* * *

ELIZABETH GLANCED at the mirror for the final time. Her skin glowed from good health and happiness. The bruises at her jaw and temple had faded to slight shadows. One of her curls covered the cut on her cheek caused by an errant tree limb. The swelling of her eye was almost gone.

She was soon to be Mrs. Fitzwilliam Darcy. Her anticipation was the opposite of how she felt when she first met him. They had gone from enemies to lovers.

"Are you nervous?" asked Jane.

Considering the question carefully, Elizabeth smoothed her skirt and then answered. "Nervous? No. Excited? Absolutely."

"Then let us go to chapel to get you wed."

* * *

DARCY'S COACHMAN painstakingly conveyed his town coach over the cart path behind the pond to Meryton. Gratefully, it was a merry and comfortable party returning to Longbourn.

Ralph and Beatrice Simmons, who attended the wedding, were overjoyed with the children. Mrs. Simmons arrived wearing a bright pink gown with pink feathers in her bonnet, making her an immediate favorite with Rebekah. When the dog first leaped from the smaller carriage that arrived behind the Simmons coach, Jake was convinced there were no better individuals on the whole earth, not even in Pennsylvania.

After the ceremony, when Mr. and Mrs. Simmons decided to take their leave, Darcy and Elizabeth chose to do the same.

"Fitzwilliam, the weather has held. Mightn't we walk to the bridge before we depart?"

He readily agreed. Hand in hand, they approached the stone bridge where the road divided.

Elizabeth plucked a leaf from an overhanging tree, dropping it into the water. "Who knew that fourteen years after a handsome lad tried to rescue me from the *HMS Voyager*, I would become his wife?"

He chuckled, pulling her close. "I am grateful you never made it to the Amazon. Your discovering Pizarro's treasure would have drawn the attention of worthier men than me. I would have lost you before I found you."

She kissed his chin. "I cannot conceive of a worthier man than you."

"Which is as it should be." He kissed her properly. "Since I found my own treasure here on this spot, this will forever be my river of dreams."

"Our river of dreams."

The water still flowed quickly, though not as fast as that day they spent on the river. He could not see the bottom, which increased his tension. He had other things to fill his mind, and his time was far more important than his fears.

"Come, my bride. Let us start our grand adventure."

Confidently putting her hand in his, she stepped into his carriage without looking back.

***

THE FIRST THREE days of their marriage were blissful. As Richard requested, Darcy found a woman who pleased him during the day and pleasured him at night. Elizabeth was in every way a delight.

As they planned, once they arrived at the outskirts of London, they hung the black wreaths on the door of Darcy's coach and transferred to a rented hack to enter the city. To facilitate Darcy's plan of action, it was important that others outside his house believe he was still missing.

On day four, Richard entered Darcy House through the kitchen entrance. Accompanying him was a man Darcy never expected to see, Mr. Arthur Pierce.

Elizabeth offered their guest the most comfortable seat in their private sitting room. "Please accept my sincerest appreciation for rescuing and caring for my husband, sir."

The man blushed. "Had my fear not overcome me, I should have made arrangements for his travel rather than allowing him to walk out alone."

Darcy asked, "Did you bring it with you?"

"I did." From a massive leather pouch that he placed on the table in front of him, Mr. Pierce pulled out a large book. "Before I hand this over, you three should know my true name is Calvin Van der Berg. My ancestors helped Johannes Gutenberg with the cost to build his first printing press. A distant uncle, Johan Fust, kept the first of the one hundred eighty volumes of the Holy Bible, which were printed on that same press in 1452. This particular tome contained scribal notes from early translators. It was priceless. To restore this treasure to my family after it was stolen sometime during the past three hundred years, I mortgaged everything to purchase from Lord Matlock my family's copy. The transaction was completed, and I returned to my domicile only to discover the paper was too new and the ink too modern to be an original. Additionally, there were no notes. It was a counterfeit."

"We shall recover what we can of your funds," Darcy promised. "Much depends on how much access Viscount Smithton has to his father's accounts. We will do our best, this I promise you."

Richard asked, "This gives us four pieces to a large puzzle of indeterminate size. Is it enough?"

Darcy replied, "With this Bible, Mr. Bennet's map, the Venus we had returned from Lord Haversham, and the golden bowl from Miles Brownly, we should be able to make a sizable dent in the Matlock's coffers."

Mr. Van der Berg sat forward in his chair. "Prince George should be your next victim. He purchased at a premium a host of items. There were books, statues, and precious jewels on the table when I returned with the funds I needed to get the Bible. When my curiosity got the best of me, Lord Matlock told me they were for someone who carried far more weight in the government than a businessman like me. I later learned from a scholar that Prince George had a desired volume from the library of Alexandria. I instantly knew it was from Lord Matlock since it was one that I saw on the table."

Darcy's brows almost shot to his hairline, as did Elizabeth's and Richard's.

"*Blast and damnation!* Only my father would be bold enough to rob the reigning sovereign of England." Richard was disgusted.

"We need a plan," Elizabeth murmured.

Darcy sat back. "I know exactly what needs to be done."

CHAPTER 24

Subtlety did not come naturally to Richard Fitzwilliam. During their lifetime, Darcy typically was the one who urged caution. However, this time, he was the first to enter the private domicile of George Augustus Frederick, the forty-nine-year-old Prince Regent of England.

"What are you doing here? Guards!" The former Prince of Wales lounged on a chaise behind a table laden with plates of pastries, fruit, sliced meats, and more bottles of wine than Darcy cared to count.

Richard, dressed in black as was Darcy, bowed low. "Your Royal Highness, our matter is urgent."

"Who are you? How did you get past my guards?"

Richard answered. "I am the second son of Lord Matlock, Colonel Richard Fitzwilliam at your service. My cousin is Fitzwilliam Darcy of Pemberley in Derbyshire."

"You used your father's name to get past my guards!" The prince pointed at them. "Guards!"

"I did."

Darcy quickly said, "I beg your pardon for interrupting

your meal, but we have an abundance of proof that Lord Matlock stole from you and others."

"What? Hugh Fitzwilliam is one of the most powerful men in my cabinet. He would never…"

Darcy hurried to state his claim. "The books from the library of Alexandria, the marbles from Greek ruins, and the statue of the goddess of love and beauty, Venus, are all copies made by skilled artisans hired by Lord Matlock." Noting the confusion on the prince's face, he continued. "For decades, my uncle has unscrupulously sold counterfeit antiques for exorbitant prices to trusting individuals who later were charged astronomical fees as interest. If they could not pay, they were sent to Marshalsea, whereupon my uncle seized all assets, inflicting immense pain and suffering on the families. He has done this with seeming impunity."

"What?" The prince jumped to his feet. "I paid a small fortune for those items."

Richard nodded. "Yes, you did. As have others. I have gathered as many items as possible from good families who trusted the wrong man."

"What did you do with them?"

Darcy replied, "I sold them to my cousin, Viscount Smithton, as originals. In this way, I claimed the money that was returned to those poor victims, and Frederick Fitzwilliam was able to impress his father with his valuable finds."

"Where is he?"

Darcy replied, "Viscount Smithton is at Matlock House. Hugh Fitzwilliam is currently at Pemberley, my estate in Derbyshire, where he is attempting to steal me blind. You see, once he heard that I died in a boating accident, he rushed to my home to claim my assets for his own. My arrival in Town seven days ago was discreet. After our appearance here, no doubt, my uncle will be informed that I am alive."

The prince rubbed his jaw. "He will be made to pay."

"We hope so, Your Royal Highness." Darcy handed the prince a folded piece of paper. "Here listed are the names of the debtors I know. It is long but certainly not complete. Viscount Smithton is quickly draining the family coffers, which will throw Lord Matlock into a panic. He will need to make money quickly. If I could suggest…"

"Continue."

"Now, while he is vulnerable, would be the perfect time for you to seek justice."

The prince took on the look of a predator. "I will ruin him. I will strip him bare as he has done others in the Kingdom. I will have his downfall placed in all the newspapers. He will be a laughingstock, never able to show his face in London again." He stopped. "But what of you? As his family, your uncle's fall will affect you."

Darcy said, "We have considered this, Your Royal Highness. It is true what you say. Nevertheless, justice and fairness must be served. My wife's father was bilked by my uncle, barely escaping debtors' prison. If this means living quietly in Derbyshire for the rest of our lives, we will do this with no regrets."

The prince shook his head. "In front of me are honorable men." He looked at each of them directly. "I will act immediately. I will make this right. You are dismissed."

It was not until they were outside the royal residence that Darcy felt the sweat running down the middle of his back. Relief that this would soon be over surged through him. He needed his safe place. He needed Elizabeth.

* * *

Until they heard from the prince's secretary, Darcy, Elizabeth, and Richard were on pins and needles. Mr. Van der Berg took his money from Freddy Fitzwilliam and returned to the Netherlands. Since he used the money from the sale of books to repay local creditors, her papa set aside a tidy sum for his wife and each of his daughters, vowing after hearing of Mr. Collins that he would take better care of himself so as not to leave them at the mercy of his heir.

Elizabeth cried in gratitude at all that her brave husband and Richard had accomplished.

Two days after Darcy and Richard snuck inside the prince's residence, a note from the prince himself arrived. It was their signal.

From the minute her husband announced the plan, the housekeeper and Elizabeth rummaged through the gowns left behind by Georgiana and Lady Anne Darcy in search of something appropriate for the occasion. As the maid put the finishing touches to her hair, Darcy entered her chambers carrying a silk-covered case containing a parure of sapphires set in platinum.

"You are the most beautiful woman in the world, Elizabeth Darcy." He kissed her bare shoulder before fastening the heavy necklace. When he held up the tiara, she shook her head "no." Instead, ten sapphire and diamond-encrusted hairpins were tucked carefully amidst her curls. Taking her fingers in his, he touched his lips to each knuckle before wrapping a bracelet around her wrist.

Once the earrings were fastened, she stood and turned toward him. Darcy was stunning in formal attire; his silver and sapphire waistcoat with the pin matching her jewelry at his cravat made his blue eyes even darker.

"I shall be escorted to the theater by the handsomest man in the world, my husband."

He wrapped her shawl around her shoulders. "We are to be noticed tonight, Elizabeth. Prince George wants London to know I am alive before the news of my uncle's downfall hits the papers early tomorrow morning. The larger stir we create by my being in the royal box at the theater, the sooner we can be done with this."

Placing her hand around his elbow, she smiled at the man alongside her. "We may be in company with Prince George, my dear, but know that you will always be the king of my heart."

"As you are my queen."

EPILOGUE

*E*lizabeth slid her bare foot down the side of Darcy's calf. Her fingers tangled in the dark hair covering his chest. With every movement, tingles ran up and down his spine.

Since their wedding night almost a year before, he had never completely relaxed until she was in his embrace.

"My love," she softly spoke.

Darcy was in that lovely place between wake and sleep. He was warm, sated, and happier than he ever could have imagined.

"Richard is here. I hear him down the stairs," she whispered in his ear, blowing softly to punctuate her sentence.

Darcy kept his eyes closed, pretending they would be allowed their privacy. "Then we will move from these chambers to the far end of the hall, so we never hear his arrival again."

She chuckled. "Come, husband. We have rested enough."

He groaned, knowing she meant their cuddle time was over.

Thirty minutes later, he entered his study to find Richard

sitting behind his desk, his booted ankles resting on the blotter.

"Get your feet off my desk." Darcy barked, noting his carafe of fine brandy was already open. "Why are you here?"

Richard smirked. "You pretend to be angry, Darcy. Well, you can stop now since I am the one who has reason to be highly irritated."

The prior year had wrought much change to the large estates in Derbyshire. In a fit of wrath, Hugh Fitzwilliam destroyed some of the Darcy family's priceless heirlooms when he learned he would not be gaining oversight of Pemberley. Later, when the prince called him to London, his uncle was given the choice to return all the money charged to his victims, including the prince himself, or transportation to Australia. When he discovered his eldest son had depleted his accounts, Hugh Fitzwilliam implicated his sister, Lady Catherine, in his crimes. The two negotiated a new start in the Americas instead of a permanent home in the South Pacific. Freddy Fitzwilliam, with no means of supporting himself, went with them.

Richard lost his commission in the military and gained the new title of Lord Matlock. Unfortunately, the Matlock holdings in Derbyshire were seized by the crown as repayment for debts against the Prince Regent. Since then, every time the prince believed someone else was attempting to take advantage, Richard was required to rush to London or Brighton, wherever the prince resided.

"What now?" Darcy asked, genuinely concerned for his cousin.

Richard harrumphed. "I received a proposal of marriage."

"What?" Darcy was stunned. What decent woman would boldly offer for a gentleman? It simply was not done.

Darcy studied his cousin closely. When Richard's countenance went from ire to softness, Darcy knew he could relax. Whoever it was, it was not displeasing to his cousin.

"While I was at Prinny's beck and call, I was sent to a small village in Berkshire where a snippet of a girl with a powerful lisp and two missing front teeth decided that since you were no longer available, she would settle for me."

"Rebekah," Darcy grinned.

"Yes. You will be pleased to know that the children are well-dressed, healthy, active, and happy. Mr. and Mrs. Simmons are delighted to have their house filled with noise and dog hair."

"Thank you. Elizabeth will be happy to hear they are well settled. I am also pleased. Now, tell me what is happening, for it cannot be two young ones that brought you to Derbyshire."

"For my loyal service this year, Prinny gave me Matlock, free and clear."

Darcy whistled under his breath. "It is your home, Richard."

Richard emptied his snifter, then began pacing.

"The house is too big. There are too many memories, few of them good. I have never managed a property before."

Darcy offered, "If Bingley can do it, then you can as well."

Richard made four trips back and forth across the carpets before he said, "Bingley's estate is half the size of Matlock, he has a wife trained to run a household, and you hired the servants."

"You know I will help you if I can," Darcy readily reminded him. "What is the real issue, Cousin?"

"Bingley has his Jane. You have your Elizabeth. Jake and Rebekah have their new family, and I am alone."

Darcy understood, easily remembering his life before Elizabeth.

"Then here is what you need to do." Taking a sip of coffee,

the memories flowed freely. "Find a stone bridge over a waterway. Wait until a lady crosses. If she ignores the river, then discard her as a potential wife. However, if she plucks a leaf from a tree or picks up a stick from the ground only to lean over and drop it over the edge, marry her. Then, you will have someone who delights your days and pleasures you at night."

Not four months later, Richard did precisely that. Miss Melinda Hanson stood gazing into the river Derwent when Richard's carriage crossed the stone bridge. The driver was distracted, causing the conveyance to get too close. His cousin rushed from the moving carriage to rescue the fair lady out of the water. In doing so, he found his own river of dreams.

The End

MISCELLANEOUS

Have you read the first book in the "Dreaming of Darcy" series: *Field of Dreams*? Reviews have been wonderful. Please, after reviewing this story, feel free to check out *Field of Dreams*, available at Amazon.

NOTES:

1. Was it common during the period for fake artifacts and antiques to be sold to the wealthy? Unfortunately, yes it was. As well, the passing of counterfeit money was rampant. If you type "forgery during the regency era" in any Internet search engine, you will read startling facts of history where many individuals were punished with a sentence of death. In my story, Lord Matlock and his son got off with a much lesser sentence.
2. Historical records indicate that the information Mr. Darcy shares with Mr. Bingley about the weather of 1810 was accurate. In fact, it was this

particular research that gave me the idea for this story.
3. I also had to research the volume of water, the speed floodwaters travel, and the buoyancy of a skiff on floodwaters before I could write the story. Mr. Darcy's estimates of how far they would have traveled are as accurate as I could make it.

ABOUT THE AUTHOR
ABOUT THE AUTHOR

Joy Dawn King fell in love with Jane Austen's writings in 2012 and discovered the world of fan fiction shortly after. Intrigued with the many possibilities, she began developing her own story for Fitzwilliam Darcy and Elizabeth Bennet. Her first book, *A Father's Sins*, was published in 2014.

In 2017, she experimented with shorter Pride & Prejudice variations using the pen name, Christie Capps.

Joy, and her beloved husband of over 40 years, live in Oregon where she often FaceTime's her daughter, author Jennifer Joy, so they can talk about grandkids, writing, and Jane Austen.

The author is currently working on another tale of adventure and romance for Mr. Darcy and his Elizabeth.

ALSO, BY J. DAWN KING

AVAILABLE FROM J Dawn King:
- *Friends and Enemies*
- *Mr. Darcy's Mail-Order Bride*
- *Love Letters from Mr. Darcy*
- *The Abominable Mr. Darcy*
- *Yes, Mr. Darcy*
- *Compromised!*
- *One Love, Two Hearts, Three Stories*
- *A Father's Sins*
- *Letter of the Law*
- *A Baby for Mr. Darcy*
- *The Long Journey Home*
- *Mistaken Identity*
- *Field of Dreams*

ALSO, BY J. DAWN KING

AVAILABLE FROM CHRISTIE CAPPS:
Mr. Darcy's Bad Day
For Pemberley
The Perfect Gift
Forever Love
Boxed Set: *Something Old, New, Later, True*
Elizabeth
Lost and Found
Henry
His Frozen Heart
Boxed Set: *Something Regency, Romantic, Rollicking, Reflective*
One Bride & Two Grooms
A Reason to Hope
Mischief & Mayhem
The Matchmaker
Boxed Set: *Something Priceless, Perilous, Precious, Playful*

THANK YOU!

Thank you very much for investing your time in this story. A gift for any author is to receive an honest review from readers. I hope you will use this opportunity to let others know your opinion.

Printed in Great Britain
by Amazon